SONIA

THE ROMANCING OF A LADY

R. CICERO

author HOUSE

AuthorHouse™
1663 Liberty Drive
Bloomington, IN 47403
www.authorhouse.com
Phone: 833-262-8899

Published by AuthorHouse 04/25/2023

ISBN: 979-8-8230-0535-7 (sc)
ISBN: 979-8-8230-0533-3 (hc)
ISBN: 979-8-8230-0534-0 (e)

Library of Congress Control Number: 2023906472

Print information available on the last page.

CHAPTER 1

As Sonia left on her next trip, her mind wandered, as always, while she sat at the Airport gate. With her ever professional presentation, men would look, but she never gave them a second look in return. She chalked it up to her conservative Catholic upbringing combined with the scar of that one killer relationship. It wasn't a lack of interest; the distraction was simply unwanted. Today, this one Mediterranean fella *had* to sit across from her, equally focused on his travels but *his* presence created a distraction that was overwhelming.

She "focused" on her presentation prep she couldn't help catching a glance at *him* at every chance. Suddenly, *he* was gone, disappointed she returned to her lecture prep. As a psychology professor she had to stay in the game at all times. This current project was for a unique allied government Intel agency.

She so disliked this part of her profession and her past, but it formed the foundation of her work. Her mastery of human source collection was uncanny, but something felt invasive at the thought of that now. This became her greatest art since her initial recruitment in college. As she began the meat of her rehearsal, the call to board was announced.

Within moments she found herself settled into First Class comfort. As she became situated in the window seat, a curious and unique Eastern European man moved into the aisle seat. Quiet at first, until he began to work and muttered in anger. She tried to ignore him, but she caught pieces of his rage at the "security issue" he referenced. This is a cost of her previous life, the craving to start a conversation that she knew would only lead to information she didn't want to know.

Just as the door was about to close, *that man* appeared, it was *him* again, that dark, evocative man. Then where did he sit, but behind her in the aisle. Again the distraction returned and her mind raced, maybe it was the celibacy of her lifestyle or his cologne. Nevermind, back to work; the plane rumbled into the air.

In time she nodded off, out of character, but it was the only way to clear the distraction of *that man* and the craving to climb into her neighbor's mind. Drifting into dreamland a strange vibration resonated through her head. Trying to make sense of it, she focused deeply, she felt close to it, and then, it was gone, back to slumber in an instant. Before she knew it, there was an announcement, they were nearly an hour from landing. A moment of planning kicked in, a trip to the restroom was a must. She tried to nudge her sleeping neighbor; he remained silent, forcing her to climb over.

And, there *he* is. They made eye contact for the first time, a strangely deep gaze. As she paused, an electric shock ran through her loins for the first time in years. A smile rose, she stumbled and nearly fell. He reached for her and caught her effortlessly. Collecting herself she ran to the restroom. As she slid out of her pants, her freshly dampened panties clung like glue and brought her mind to a place not indulged in years. An ache burned. It could not be tended to.

As she prayed for a distraction, a scream from the cabin did it. Reassembling herself she returned to her seat to find the crew securing the area. One of the attendants directed her to another seat, advising her the man next to her had died. Her thoughts turned to who was he? how did he die? would they consider her a suspect???

The attendants did question her briefly, but not in any detail, and certainly not like she would have. In short order, they were on the ground and greeted by local authorities. She was ushered by a handler, and escorted to a car by US and Allied Authorities. As she relaxed in their security she glanced over to see the object of her obsession getting into a similar vehicle. Damn, who is *he*, was he watching her, or was he watching over her?! South America is no longer a stable, safe place for Americans, how are they connected? In moments, his vehicle changed directions from hers, clearing her mind back to work.

She was off to the conference where she was treated like a Queen. She was guided to an office with a fresh, light, but full meal waiting for her and several others. In a blink came the Ambassador, Station Chief, Deputy Prime Minister, and several assistants. As the Station Chief passed, he whispered "your Ukrainian seatmate had a massive stroke. Don't sweat it, FYI, he was old KGB too."

With a sigh of relief, she was able to ignore the banter and on to the GAME. Entering the auditorium, she was the rock star, all eyes and ears were on her every word. She held them in every second and ruled the room like she was climbing into every mind present. Then, *those* eyes met hers, damn it. Who is *he*? In all of the years at the Agency and alike, they never crossed paths until today and here *he* was, at every turn. She glided through and was whisked off to several high level meetings, which cleared her head for the rest of the day. Finally, she was off to the hotel.

Upon arrival at the Hotel Intercontinental the pampering began with a long needed nap followed by a nice hot bath. As she stripped *those* eyes popped into her head like she was stripping for *him*! In the tub all she could think of was *him* touching her like the water and bubbles. Her fingers ran over her body slowly and deliberately, down her neck and into her cleavage. With a deep breath, a full breast filled her hand, a nipple pinch and a roll in her finger tips. As her legs rubbed together, the frustrations of her day erupted in a blink as she touched her clitoris. In a torrent her hands and fingers panicked, as they sought to bring a final release of the day! Gasping, trembling, "Lord YES!" she thought; then an alarm sounded, reminding her of a dinner meeting in just 45 minutes.

A rush to dry, prep and dress, is paused as she searches for panties in her bag. "Really? how did I forget panties?" she thought. No time to wonder about that, she slid into her silk stockings and garter belt, a favorite little dress and heals. She ran to the hotel restaurant. As she entered, her long time friend Lucinda waved from the bar. In a warm embrace, they exchanged cheek kisses and huge smiles. Three years of catching up began with a classic Mojito and amazing appetizers. As they giggled, Lucinda noticed a sharp looking man at the bar, "Sonia, would you look at *that* all alone? You know I have been celibate since my divorce…would you, you know?" Sonia glanced over, "Really? *him* again, he is definitely assigned to me…" she thought. Then exclaimed "No way! "He was on the plane with me and all he did was fart and hit on me".

"Well, did he stink?! I would like him to do much more than just 'hit' on me! You do remember other girls still have needs, you need to get over wimpy old what's his name," replied Lucinda. In an instant Lucinda was on her feet strutting toward him, motioning for Sonia to follow. Sonia caught up just as Lucinda softly touched *his* shoulder and warmly greeted "hola, hombre".

He responded in English, "good evening ladies I don't know how I could be so lucky, my name is Ricco. I am here for the next few days on business, but it would be nice to get to know you." The same scent from the airplane filled the ladies lungs and brought a smile to their faces. Sonia started to melt again, as the same thoughts raced from the plane and the bath. As they exchanged introductions, a large group entered the lounge and created quite a loud disturbance. Ricco immediately stood and addressed the matter. When he returned, Sonia inquired if he was staying at the Hotel. He nodded yes, and to Lucinda's surprise she suggested they all get a round of drinks and go to his room for a quiet room service dinner. They agreed with a warm hug, Ricco took the liberty of ordering: a bottle of Chianti, oysters, shrimp, brochette and a Charcuterie board for *his* room.

As they moved to the elevator the ladies moved to either side of him. Without a word, he pressed the top floor button and he held it to override other floor stops. As the car slightly jerked Lucinda fell into his arms, with broad smiles they were nose to nose. As a gentleman, Ricco gently kissed her cheek and leaned back, he couldn't help but notice the look in Sonia's eyes as she bit her lip and squeezed her knees together. In a moment, the doors opened. Without a word, he took the ladies by the hand and to his door.

As the door opened, both women took note of how tidy and organized the room was, unlike most travelers, and how only one side of the bed was turned down. Sonia excused herself to the bathroom, the reality of no panties was a hot wet trail running down her thighs collecting in her stockings, "they have to come off", she thought, as her mind raced. Slipping each wet silk hose down her leg only increased her excitement. With the straps of her garter belt dangling, she entered the room just as the food was being delivered. What a welcome distraction, food would satisfy her for the moment!

As they sat at the table, Lucinda fed Ricco an oyster in the most seductive manner.

Little did Sonia know just moments earlier they had been kissing passionately and Lucinda had released her first wave of pleasure. Before they knew it they all were feeding each other and sharing drinks in the most provocative way. As they finished the great meal Lucinda shifted in her seat to reveal her raised hemline and bare delight. With a grin, she ran her fingers through Ricco's hair inquiring " Are you ready for dessert?" Sonia clutched her breast and felt her body tremble, she never knew this side of Lucinda and would never have pictured herself in this position. Ricco dropped to his knees, Sonia gasped in excitement and surprise; she was about to witness something unlike anything she had ever imagined. As his lips hit Lucinda's lower lips, Sonia nearly burst in anticipation. She lost her normal, cool demeanor and rose to her feet. She ran to the elevator.

She prayed for the car to be empty, but the doors opened, revealing an older, reserved couple. Anxiously and silently, she pressed the button. The seconds were like hours as the steaming honey ran down her legs, the elevator opened to allow her the effort of escape. As she opened her door she fell to the bed, her hand cupping her boiling vault, frantically working toward an earth shaking quake. As she began to recover, another need struck and could only be filled as her finger tips probed deeper and deeper. She was brought to a huge rush. What had come over her? How had this lust taken over her very controlled life? She shed her wet clothes, taking stock of the beauty that she tried to suppress. She began to recognize what years of neglect was doing to her needs.

A hot shower and much needed meditation finally calmed her inferno. As she slid into bed naked (which she never did), her mind drifted to Lucinda and *that* man, *Ricco*. Her thoughts raced again. What had she missed out on? Would it have been wrong to stay? She had never thought of her friend in that way. Oh! what passion she had never imagined, this trip had to end, and fast.

CHAPTER 2

Hours later, thunderous knocking began at her door, "What the?!" she thought. " Hold on", she said in English and Spanish, "Hurry!!!" a man's voice said. As she slid on the thick fluffy robe, the authoritative voice said "This is an urgent matter, you have to get moving!" As she cracked the door there *he* was again! Smelling of sex and all! "Really?" she thought. "Get dressed, grab your stuff. We have to get on a plane, Lucinda is already moving with Embassy personnel." Seeing her expression, he continued, "Look, get moving, I will tell you all you need to know, you are not leaving my sight. Is that clear?!"

To her dismay, this was very real.The robe dropped as she jumped into jeans and sneakers, ignoring how her bare ass glistened. The obvious urgency forced her to ignore her modesty and emotions, Ricco threw her discarded items into her bag. His phone chirped, he glanced quickly and said "Now! Leave the rest!" Her hand in his, he threw the door open and drew his pistol, rushing down the hall, he pushed her into a doorway to cover her. Two shots rang out, she ran in his direction and followed him down the fire stairs to a waiting sedan. He threw her into the open back seat and jumped in the open front door, "Stay down!" he exclaimed. She heard something hitting the car just before the rear window burst. He began shooting over her out the back window as they sped off. In a blink he drug her from the car to a running jet with armed men surrounding it. Her mind spun, this was never part of her life!

They sprinted to the plane, Embassy staff were already seated. The security team boarded and they were off, without even being seated. Ricco kissed her forehead and ran to the cockpit. Hours later the passengers had calmed and were making conversation, but not even the Ambassador knew what had happened. Ricco emerged standing like a General at the front of the plane, "Ladies and gentlemen, please take a breath and relax. There was an incident organized by Eastern European elements to conduct an assassination. We have had complete success in your evacuation. Please enjoy the drinks and snacks the team is offering, we will be in Miami in two hours." Sonia tried to relax, her thoughts a jumble, "What was last night? The man on the plane? Why her?" Lucinda leaned over, "Are you mad at me?"she asked. "Of course not Sonia responded, "I just wasn't prepared and never...... (sigh) Was it good?" Lucinda smiled and replied. "Ummmm I am sore in an amazing way and wow... He said I will likely never see him again."

"Ladies and gentlemen, please prepare for landing. Upon arrival, you all will be separated and interviewed," the intercom voice said. They were serious, as soon as the plane came to a stop, they were all whisked away in individual vehicles. Sonia was escorted to a dimly lit room in a huge Air Force Building. No sooner had she sat down when *he* entered the room shutting the door. "Sonia Bianci, it is nice to finally meet you professionally. You have caused quite a stir. You are in no trouble, but there is a 'rat in the wood pile' trying to sell you and your skills. Until this is sorted out you are stuck with me! Yes, my name is actually Rick, and you are my mission!" He sat across from her, "Sorry about last night, it was the best way to ensure where you would be, and yes, you are a beautiful lady but the mission took precedence." She felt totally confused, honored, respected, appreciated and insulted all at once. Was her desire in vain or was this just a mission focused soldier they write about?

"Can I ask some questions?" she inquired. He replied, "Certainly, but I may not be able to answer them. Yes, I would have loved to. No I wouldn't have, not then. You are the mission. Were those your questions?" His tone was serious. She did not answer, except for a deep sigh as she put her head in her hands.

"Let's get you out of here, I have a great place on the beach," he said, returning to that seductive tone. "Really? I am so confused," she thought as she took his hand, moving toward a classic Camaro. He came around to her side first. She was surprised, and thought "He opens doors and closes them too? what the ...."

A short ride took them to a secluded walled home not far from the beach, she loved the sound of the water. He guided her to her room, offering small talk, which she ignored. In the room was an assortment of her clothes, shoes and personal items. "How?" she asked.

"You may not realize it but you are an important asset! Please get comfortable, your favorite items are in the bath and plenty of fresh towels. Do you like Alfredo sauce and Balsamic Chicken?" He offered. She shrugged, exhausted, and he left for the kitchen.

"What have I gotten myself into? All of these years I just wanted to put my skills to good use and help my county." She said aloud. As she stripped, the reality returned, no bra as her full breasts swayed, and no panties. "Damn it! What is going on?" she thought. A polite knock was followed by the door cracking and a glass of white wine being placed on the table.

As she basqued in the shower, the aroma of dinner filled the house, "And he cooks" she thought. Another knock was followed by "Dinner in 10".

She jumped like a schoolgirl, drying, throwing her hair up and jumping into a little dress. "Oh shit, panties! Nevermind, he wouldn't if I offered...Damn it!" she said to herself. Into the kitchen she bounced, displaying her empty glass. Without a word, he filled it and smiled. On the table was homemade Fettuccine Alfredo, perfectly spiced chicken and garlic bread. Again with the small talk, he prepared her plate, she ignored him, yet again. "Just so you know I *can* be a nice guy, but if you continue to be rude...." he advised. "I am just trying to protect myself, I am sorry. You are a man of a different breed. You scare me and attract me all at the same time. What should I do?" She asked.

"Be a good person. Be good to me and I will keep you safe! Let's enjoy a great dinner." He replied. She smiled and savored every bite, as she used her bread to get the last drop of sauce she asked "Do you always cook like this?" With an even bigger smile Rick replied "When I have the right reasons, and when I do, it feels wonderful." She suddenly realized her toes were sliding up and down his leg. In embarrassment, she pulled back and blushed, her nipples stiff against her dress. That could not be hidden.

"This is the best, hardest mission I have ever had. Let's have some dessert", he suggested, as he offered still warm Tapioca Pudding. "I have loved this my entire life!" she exclaimed.

After dinner she felt relaxed. She took over cleaning up and danced as she worked to the old "Rat Pack" music playing. As he tried to complete his reports, she was a great distraction. His phone rang, and to his room he ran. "Wait? What? Why?This is the most confusing excitement ever." she thought as she went to her room and tried to read.

Hours passed and she nodded off. Dreams of every nature filled her head, interrupted by thoughts "What could have happened with those men? Was it him trying to sell her off?"and then went back to sleep. Deep in slumber, a crash of thunder threw her from the bed to her feet. Without even thinking she ran to his room and jumped into his bed, like a frightened child. "I am sorry, please just hold me so I know I am safe" she pleaded. "Shhhhhhh" he said, as he caressed her cheek and kissed her forehead. She guided his hand to her waist and snuggled close to him.

Hours later he woke, trying not to disturb her, he peeled her from him and slid out of bed. She was not quite asleep, and as he walked to the washroom she admired his naked outline in the dim light. He had been naked all night and never took advantage of her, this guy is *something*, she observed silently.

Her mind wandered, so did her fingers as the silk teased her skin. "Screw it!" she thought. She rose, shedding her little silk gown as she moved through the room, past the steam, and into his shower. "I know you have your orders, but please!" She said, as she fell into his chest, melting her body to his, those strong hands roamed her flesh. "It has been so long," she whispered in his ear. Her small hands found that fat prize, which was beyond her imaginings, she wrapped her fingers around and squeezed firmly. Pushing him back to the seat, it stood there proud, calling her. No words were exchanged as she straddled and took it inch by inch. Her steaming slick flow covering them both, as her first trembling grew to a low howl of pleasure. A kiss as hot as their union finally happened, like an injection of rocket fuel to her desire, she erupted in steaming waves of ecstasy. Without warning, she collapsed to the floor, grasping that fat cock and inhaling it, feeding like a starved animal. In seconds she had the gush she craved, extracting and swallowing every drop.

"You know this must be our secret in every way!" he explained. "Oh it will be, the more I want you, the more everyone will think I hate you" she answered coyly. *Oh what a partnership we will have*, they both thought, and she kissed her way up his body. Petting, caressing and tenderly washing each other consumed them, until his phone barked, literally.

"Hurry up!" the ring tone sounded like a Drill Sergeant saying, "Hurry Up!" "Oh shit, we have to get moving, we have quite a day ahead," as he ran to answer. "Yes sir, we are getting ready now, what time does the bird leave? Yes sir" He replied.

As she dried, it teased him horribly. He wanted nothing more than to spend the day consumed by each other. He selected her outfit: black slacks, black pumps, a white silk blouse and a black jacket. For himself, he chose a business suit, tie, two guns and four magazines. Grabbing their two prepped bags, he said, "Off to DC, my lady!" Into that cool red Camaro they climbed, and they were off.

She wanted to touch him constantly and couldn't help the constant small talk now. "One question, when do I get panties?" she quibbled. "You didn't pack any, so I thought you didn't like them, sorry" he replied with a smile. "If what I am feeling continues I won't!" she proclaimed.

At the airfield, they were welcomed to the plane by uniformed personnel and escorted to a private area in the tail section. Two large reclining seats, video monitors and morning coffee were waiting for them. As they became comfortable, the plane taxied and off they went. He couldn't resist sliding his fingers up and down the supple skin of her arm and hand; knowing it made her squirm was even better. Moments later a young female Flight Attendant entered, Sonia yelled how disgusted she was to be saddled with Ricco as a babysitter. The young woman giggled and said to RIck, "When you get released from the queen you can be *my* keeper!" He smiled as she placed their breakfasts with an extra wiggle of her tush as she left.

Sonia giggled, kicking off a shoe, rubbing her bare foot on his leg and licking her lips. As they finished their meal, she smiled, and her hand slid into her slacks. With a wiggle she removed two glistening fingers, offering them at his lips! As he relished the taste, the door cracked again, she quickly pulled her hand back. As the tray was collected it was evident her pants were open when the young woman winked. As she exited, she made it clear, "I will leave you alone unless there is something you need, then don't hesitate to buzz me." She shut the door to their compartment as she went.

With the door clicking, Rick dropped to his knees, pulling her pants by the cuffs to slide them off in one tug. Sonia threw her bare legs to the sky to offer her sweet blessing, so little and sensitive. As that talented tongue tended to her clitoris Sonia found a pillow to muffle her squeals. He rose to kiss her intensely, then the voice on the speaker advised them that they were preparing to land. She jumped to get back into her slacks as the door opened. "I guess you worked it out, I'm Carla if *you* get fired" pointing at Rick. She giggled, and collected the last few items. Stopping to raise a finger to her lips as she exited "Shhhhhhhh" she reassured, and she handed Sonia a card.

Sonia raised the card to see "Carla, 813-525-2634, call me some time". "Wow, I can't believe this, it seems to me like I have really been missing out. You are going to change that aren't you? Please?"

The plane parked and they collected their items, Sonia could hardly contain her excitement. The professional face was on but the wiggle in her walk was incredible!

CHAPTER 3

As the meetings began, volumes of senior leaders entered the room taking their places at the lead table, while the other members moved to the gallery area. Sonia began to realize the gravity of what was actually happening, Generals were in the Gallery!

Rick stepped to the front of the room, "Good morning ladies and gentlemen I am codename Ricco, lead agent on the Bianci matter. We all know the critical influence Ms. Bianci has had in our operations and communications efforts over the years. Within that we have a problem in our house, I was assigned this matter when actionable Intel was first verified. Through the efforts of my team, we stopped the threatening team lead with our sonic disruptor on the aircraft without incident. When the Subject L was distracted, access to her phone verified that she was the leak as well as the intended action of the following morning. Our team successfully extracted Bianci and the Embassy Executive Team without any friendly casualties."

As Sonia listened, the depth of the situation began to unfold, how blind she had become by her "science" . She had ignored reality! This man was sent for her, and only her. She leaned to his ear, "How long will you be with me?" " As long as you need and want me" he whispered. Without a word she faked a grimace, while sensually rubbing his leg.

Her conflicting presentations were suddenly interrupted when the reality of the enemy plans was presented. The threat of being whisked away to a secluded Eastern European country, to be locked away as they delved into her secret approaches to effect a popularization of Socialism to Communism was as genuine as her need to breathe! Ricco was the only way to stop it, and he had done it.

With the enemy casualty report completed, Sonia stood, without introduction. "It is clear that everyone here knows me, but I only know a handful of you. I can't thank you enough for your bravery and efforts. I have to come to grips with a long time friend truly selling me to an enemy that I didn't know existed. Now, where do we go from here? How do we take the offensive and beat them into submission?"

A young general officer with no name tag stood, "Ms. Bianci, that is where you come in. You are the brain crasher, we are ready to support your effort with action. We have a series of trips planned for you and Ricco, these trips will center on reminding the world of the very real evils of Socialism and the end state goals they present to take from those who have worked so hard in freedom to oppress them. First, we must remind our Western Allies, who have become so weak in appeasements. The next phase is within our own society, and lastly to the countries on the cusp of transition. Do you understand your power now?"

Sonia gave pause, "I had no idea the impact of my work and the effect my appreciation of 'Social Justice' was having. I am IN, this is REAL and we MUST act."

"Agent Ricco, your required resources are packed and waiting in the vehicle out front. Please get Ms. Bianci on the plane to Paris at 14:00, you will be briefed when you meet your contact 'Mrs. Blue'." Said a booming voice. Ricco took Sonia's hand and escorted her out. As they reached the door, he gave her a wicked grin, she responded by pulling his hand to her cleavage briefly. As they approached the car, Rick opened the door guiding her in while sneaking a peek into her open blouse.

As Rick slid in, he noticed the screen was up and her blouse was open. Without a word, she slid her breasts out of her bra. In surrender, she offered them to him as they took the short ride to the airport. She had never behaved this way or enjoyed such lust. The sensations of his touch, lips, tongue and so much more made her flame burn so hot. How had she gone through her adult life without knowing such pleasure? Regaining her senses it was clear they were arriving.

With the car coming to a stop, Rick opened the door while the driver removed their bags. As Rick extended a hand to help her from the car, Sonia slammed it away exclaiming "You work *for* me, you are not *with* me" and she distanced herself from him clearly in the public moment. He smiled with a nod to move them through the crowds. Avoiding the ticket gate, he directed her to the diplomatic area. She had never experienced such treatment, she was greeted politely with a glass of champagne in exchange for their bags. She gave Rick a soft hug and she realized he still had his guns.

So many thoughts about today and what had transpired in less than 48 hours, "Was this a dream? Or the years of a fate she had been avoiding crashing into her life?" she wondered. Soon, the call to board was announced, as they moved to the escort area she felt oddly important. The plane had loaded, and they were guided to their first class seats. The Flight attendant offered blankets, pillows, a warm moist towel, and another glass of champagne with a wide smile. The inadvertent touch of her hand on Sonia's brought little shocks, what *had* happened in these past few days?!

Soon, they were in the air again, she couldn't help but curl up to him. She felt secure and protected for the first time since her father effectively left her life when she was such a young girl. "So nice" is all she could think before she drifted off to sleep. Dreams filled her thoughts with the greatest relaxation.

After a few bumps she was startled and awoke, instantly comforted when she realized she was covered in blankets and so warm next to him. Instinctively her hands roamed and she kissed his neck, his strong hand stroking her neck so gently. The reality of the darkness that had fallen reminded her of the fact of their travel. Not a word, her hand found that fat toy she was rapidly developing a craving for. Without thought of consequence she freed it and slid her mouth to it, concealed by the blankets. Using the slowest, most deliberate movements, ones she had never used before, she brought him an exceptional release. Quietly, she enjoyed every morsel of this snack, slowly abandoning and securing her prize to climb out from under the blanket.

The most satisfied expression filled her eyes as she gazed into his. "Good morning," he whispered and kissed her forehead in what was becoming a signature display of his affection. She rose from her seat to go to the restroom and met the Flight Attendant. The young lady smiled softly as she gently wiped a droplet from Sonia's chin. Raising the finger to her lips, she licked it. She cooed, "You are such a lucky lady, what a tasty snack you have had. Let me know if I can be of any assistance,"

Sonia was speechless and hurried to the bathroom. She flushed as she locked the door. As her slacks hit the floor her drenched vault couldn't be ignored, in three strokes she was shuddering in delight! Another big bump brought her back to the need to relieve her bladder. The continued bumps rushed her to return to her seat.

Upon return she found the Flight Attendant speaking with Rick, in an instant Sonia boiled with jealousy. She stopped, thinking she hasn't felt like this since she was a teen. She tried to reason with herself as she moved down the aisle, but she knew his taste and did not want to share. As she got closer the attendant turned with a smile, "Madame, I brought you coffee and warm pastry. Please, be comfortable with your husband, we will be landing soon." Husband? she hesitated, then remembered her new cover indicated she was married to Rick. What a thought, she could get used to this!

Snuggling in, she felt warm and loved for the first time in over a decade, and she was loving it. With a silent grin she pressed into him as they shared their warm treat. They finished and prepared to land, quietly rehearsing the actions on the ground for the next 48 hours. The plan was simple: get to the hotel, freshen up, move to the University and conduct the first presentation to faculty that afternoon. That evening they were to dine with the Ambassador, his staff, the French President and her staff. The second morning was the big challenge, an open presentation to students and the public, in a public arena. Preparation and flexibility is what makes for mission success.

As they exited the plane, the Intel was spot on! Paris was no longer the European Jewel of the West. Rather, it was a visibly fractured community of unhappy citizens forced to live under the desires of outsiders. Those who were once guests were now demanding control of their lives. "Hhmmmmm, this is much worse than I thought" she whispered. As they collected their luggage, Embassy escorts arrived and identified themselves, "Ricco, stay on a swivel, but you know that!" As the last bag came off the belt, they were on the move.

They loaded into the Audi, the door shut, and they were off with a jerk of the vehicle that threw her into his arms. She melted in comfort and kissed him softly, saying "To hell with looking hateful, I have to admit, I love this!" Arriving at the DeGaul International Hotel they were escorted to the Honeymoon Suite. The door opened to reveal comfort far beyond what she was used to, marble, satin and so much more. They were escorted through the room, the huge 4 poster bed, garden Jacuzzi tub, and massive shower made her wish that a leisurely week's stay had been planned. The view of Paris was stunning from every direction, what a joy.

Reality kicked in when it was evident that something had just exploded in the distance. A huge cloud of white and black smoke erupted. Sirens, horns, flashing lights, she said painfully, "Is this what has really become of beautiful Paris?" Rick grimaced and nodded, as his phone rang like an old dial phone. "Yes sir, sir, I understand, we will be ready in 30! Yes sir!"

"Sugar, we need to shake the lead out, that was at the campus. We are moving the meeting to a secured French Police facility." Rick rushed out of his clothes and ran to the shower. As he was finishing, Sonia entered with a smile, offering a warm hot kiss. "Don't hate me, I have to keep my focus, this is serious my dear", he said. She smiled, nodded and picked up her pace to match his.

She had found her business demeanor quickly and was ready to rock. They dressed and prepped in seconds now, but a brief interruption brought a new sensation to her angst. He asked, "Do you know how to shoot? This is a revolver, very simple and easy but only 6 shots," her heart sank. "I am a scientist, a doctor, not a...." she retorted. He replied, "This is getting serious, that bomb was for *you*. Come here. Stand, feet shoulder width apart, bend your knees, shoulders over knees, and push both hands out. Now, with the pistol in your hands, when you need it, put this front sight on the center of the chest and press. When we have more time we are going to do much more work, for today this is going on your left inner thigh. Raise your skirt darlin'." She obeyed, and as he knelt to affix the holster, the scent of her bare treasure filled his nose. With a big grin he smiled up into her eyes, he finished with a quick kiss on her clit. "Now FOCUS!" he said as he lowered her hem line. "It's time, let's go."

"Stay a half a step behind me from here on. If I push you down, stay that way until I yell MOVE. If I run, get on my back and stay up, no screaming. EVER. Got it?" She nodded and changed her high heels for nice little pumps. She began to notice his brief hesitation at every corner and passing entry way, she tried to replicate it in her movements. As they reached the waiting car and entered, he gave her a subtle kiss, saying, "You are a quick study."

CHAPTER 4

As they drove, she observed the difference in the residents' eyes, some terrified, others arrogant, while most appeared confused and out of their element. Sonia took every aspect into consideration for her pending presentation. Her life's work was coming to fruition, she had truly become The Authority. Reflecting on recent changes in society reminded her of why the "understanding to accept" philosophy had been so detrimental. "We MUST do what is right for the whole and not the few, we all MUST come together to work as ONE!" She longed to scream out loud, but said it only to herself.

The car came to a stop at the opening gate, they entered as soon as there was the minimum room and came to a stop with the armed detail surrounding it. "Bonjour Madame, Merci", the door opened. Rick spoke with the group leader as they moved purposefully to a conference room, he turned to her, and said "Get ready, you are on in 10. I have to get eyes, they will be there with you." Rick left with the team lead and a stern woman in a suit.

Minutes later Rick returned, "Follow me to the edge of the stage, we will remain in the shadows. Conduct your presentation as you please with a max time of 2 hours, then straight off stage with me. We will not do questions until lunch with key players." Rick was clear and concise, Sonia was confident he had her well cared for!

As she stepped onto the stage, she was more confident than ever. She stepped into the heart of the matter from the start and never wavered. Getting through 85% of her presentation, the aspect of abandoning the "acceptance approach" brought chants of "Fuck you American Capitalist Pig". Without hesitation, she grew to 10 feet tall in her presentation as she responded, "Funny, coming from a descendant of those who surrendered to the Germans and prayed we would save you. Then, after we did, you demanded gold from our resources, which we happily paid, to help you rebuild. Now sit down, shut up, and learn some history. YOU are the problem!" Silence rang through the room, heart beats were audible. "That is right, time to become mature adults and be responsible for your choices! Now assemble as ONE for your society and abandon the foolish ideals that have been pushed onto you to disrupt you from being the true French Society, Viva La France!" As she exited the stage chants of "Vive La France" filled the hall.

Meeting Rick, he ushered her to the ladies room that was secured by a female officer. She offered praise, saying, "Madame, you are such a powerful lady. Thank you!" Sonia smiled politely, but had no time to chat. As she raised her skirt, the pistol on her leg kept her locked on the gravity of the situation. She quickly relieved herself, washed her hands and did a mirror check. "Now go!" She thought and rejoined Rick to walk to the luncheon. Rick and the stern woman guided her up stairs, down several halls and into a room with a bank vault door (Holy....)

The large room was packed with men and women in suits and uniforms, there was a curtain obscuring what she believed to be a presentation. Sonia was introduced, and directed to her seat, everyone in the room had their name and title in front of them. As they began serving, the questions began. The first, from the President of the University, who demanded to know how she could have been so rude in her message. Sonia was direct and blunt, "When the ship is sinking, but *can* be saved, there is no time to complain about who or what caused it. We MUST stop the water from coming in, get as much out as we can and move to safety." The president lowered his head and quietly took his seat.

The Dean of Humanities was next. She stood, and she spoke only in French. She demanded an apology for the comments about surrendering to the Germans and having to be saved by the Americans, concluding with an admonishing reminder that Sonia was their guest. Sonia asked, "Does Humanities reflect on historical facts? The fact that the English and Canadian Forces attempted to assist the French against the Germans? That the attempts failed? That the Germans did obtain a surrender from French leadership? Furthermore, French forces in the police and other elements did, in fact, work with and under the German leadership. The small French force that returned to France with the American forces succeeded because the American Forces fought to get them there and protect them along the way. Lastly, the current situation has been created by weak leadership failing to stand up for and maintain the French way of life. Truth is seldom kind!" The woman screamed and ran from the room sobbing.

The Chief of Police stood, "You are 100% correct, but with our government and the resistance of the disrupters, how do you expect us to live as traditional French ever again?" He sat as a defeated man. Sonia was simple and kind in her response, "You have laws, *use* them. Empower your personnel to enforce them, excite the overwhelming French majority to take part. Cowardice has no place in leadership!"

The room calmed, small talk ensued and smiles began to grow. "Vive La France!" could still be heard at varied times during the conversations. As dessert was served, Rick received a notice. With that, he advised Sonia that they had to move to the arena area.

Leaving the gate, the small groups around the facility screamed "Go home Capitalist Pig!" "That woman from Humanities is the enemy you know, she would be happy to see you dead! This is going to be your greatest challenge yet. Use that same mature, direct approach, and stand tall! I have your back in every way," Rick explained.

As they drove into the stadium area there were diverse groups promoting different things, waving different flags and holding various signs. They all were Socialist themed, promoting Communist Ideology. Sonia looked at him in fear, "I had no idea this is where things had gone. I have some responsibility in this I suppose." Holding her, Rick replied, "You do, but that also makes you the perfect person to start the correction."

As they pulled in, Security was present, but much more reserved. As

Sonia was escorted from the vehicle, they remained close but were not overtly strong. She could hear mixed chanting of "Vive La France" and "Yankee Capitalist Pig". She glanced at Rick with fear filling her eyes, "Get out there, stand tall and do what you do, I am here for you" he reassured her.

They reached the stage, her game face clearly in place. "Good afternoon Paris! You are the beauty of your great city! Shine as bright as the light you carry like no other city."

Silence was followed by the first cheers, "Paris has led France as it has led Europe and the World for centuries. You must be leaders and not followers! In a world that demands of those who do, you are the doers. Stop bending to those who refuse to 'do', but instead use you to make themselves happy. Do you feed the wolf biting your leg? Or, do you get rid of it?" Quick chants of "Yankee Capitalist" were cut short as true French Patriots escorted the offenders to the exits. The gates were opened and Sonia took the lead! From that point the audience was hers. And lead she did, in every way.

Time flashed as she was given the 2 hour warning to wrap it up. "In conclusion, you have sacrificed for your country, your neighbor and your family. Never surrender to the demands of those who want to use you so they can prosper without effort or dedication!" Chants of "Vive La France" rang like a bell as she exited with cheers and waving flags. The word was out.

Moving to the car she gave Rick a quick kiss on the neck, "What have you brought out of me?" she whispered with a huge smile. He hurried her into the car and snuggled in next to her. "I guess the hate is gone?" he retorted. Without a word she kissed him with a passion that had been building for years. Grabbing a breath he exclaimed, "The DeGaul, please." They quietly snuggled up as she glowed.

At the hotel, they rushed to the room, even though they had 3 hours before dinner. It had been such a long day already. Sonia hadn't been this close to a man in 15 years, now she couldn't imagine being apart from him after only three days, three *huge* days. As he made a couple of calls, she slowly prepared to indulge in a hot bath. She prepared purposefully, hoping he would notice and join her. She gently removed her clothes in the most "lady like" way. Her amazing body was lit by the sun through the floor to ceiling windows, and he did notice. "I will be in the tub, if you..." she invited.

Lowering her body into the bubbles was so invigorating. She grabbed her razor and cream to tend to some ignored hygiene. She shaved those soft smooth legs to perfection, then there was that "wild mess" she had ignored for years. It had been hotter over the last three days than she ever remembered. Gently, she trimmed and sculpted it to a work of delicate art. Just as she rinsed, a knock preceded a glass of white wine, "Oh please!" she exclaimed. "What else do you need my lady?" he inquired. Without a word, stretched out her soft little hand and motioned with her fingers.

As he approached, she raised a breast and stiffening nipple to her lips. He shed his clothes as she tempted him with even more. Climbing into the tub, she welcomed him with every inch of her, "Make slow love to me" she said. And that, he did, with a passion she had only read and fantasized about. The hot water and bubbles made it all the more delicious. They both reached amazing bursts; they remained united, lounging in feelings neither had ever truly experienced. Their bodies moved in slow unison under the waves of the tub.

Realizing the water was cooling, they knew it was time to get back to work. The view of her body was something songs and poems are written about, he felt so blessed. Little did he know, her thoughts were the same. As they finished another couple of glasses of wine, they dressed. She displayed the low cut black dress that had been packed for her, "Bra, or no?" she asked. "No darlin', we are in Paris" he responded. Seeing her dress was as provocative as watching her strip. She raised stockings in her hand, he shook his head no as she smiled widely. Nothing between him and her but that pretty little dress!

They were quickly on the move again, he had enjoyed every minute of watching her primp and prep. She sat so proudly next to him as they rode through the city, her anxiety was all but gone. At the Embassy she moved without hesitation at every step and turn, greeting the Dignitaries, including the President, with ease. During dinner she was seated with the President, much to her dismay Rick was working, and had to remain ever vigilant.

President LaSalle was a lovely woman about her age who spoke well and was supportive of the efforts Sonia had expressed throughout the day. The Minister of Communications had another outlook. As the ladies spoke he interjected, "Just what gives you the right to be such an 'Ugly American'?" Furthermore you are starting a fire we must extinguish to please the special interests!"

Sonia took a breath, "President LaSalle is the leader as I understand it, I could be wrong but you are here to help her and the French population. Wasn't there a revolution or two in world history about taking from the people who do, to give to those who don't and yet demand? Maybe you should be replaced!" The president silently squeezed her hand, Sonia continued, "That is right, we are all here to do the right thing and stop bending to the will of those who seek to take from those who make life possible." Sonia held nothing back, President LaSalle whispered, "Can I hire you?" The ladies smiled and continued dinner as those who sought to derail the visit sat quietly.

As dinner was completed, the Ambassador, the President and other key personnel moved to the Ambassador's office. As the door closed a document was passed to everyone in attendance. Opening the cover sheets, they read silently, President LaSalle covered her mouth in fear. Ambassador Cheval stood, "Ladies and gentlemen, this is a real threat to the ways of life in our western countries. There is no longer time for debate or discussion, rather, a time for action. As you see, there are armed elements seeking to take aggressive actions on the leadership and key personnel in our countries. Are we all in on this together?"

President LaSalle gazed, she was somber and sincere. "I understood there was a problem, but it was not presented in the clear, immediate fashion I see here. We will act to stop these efforts in the restricted areas and the autonomous aspects we have been permitting. It will be hard but I see the French Society has been calling for it and we have been failing. Thank you, thank you all. Ms. Bianci, you have set the climate in the right direction."

Moments later it was time to end and return to the hotel for the night. They were traveling to London in the morning. In the car Sonia softly kissed Rick with tenderness and true affection, not a word was needed. They sat quietly and comfortably in each other's arms like a couple that was meant for the ages.

Once at the hotel they were blessed with an empty elevator, she collapsed into the slow, deep kiss she had been longing for. In moments the doors opened, forcing them to break their embrace. Happiness filled her like never before, as the door opened to the room she ran to the bed as a willing subject. Her hem rose as if by command, he dropped to his knee, as her servant. When his lips hit her ankle an electric shock went through her. With his hot lips tracing her inner thighs the desire held her like chains. Wanting to clutch him but powerless to act other than enjoy the pampering. That tongue became magnetic at her clitoris, licking, flicking, taunting, but when those lips sucked she lost all control. Her legs clinched, heels digging into his back as one hand grabbed his head the other milking a breast. With her body in full gear, she swelled with joy, drowning him in her sweet nectar.

Pulling him to her hungry mouth she inhaled his tongue drenched in her, she felt his hardness press at her gate. Instinctively she opened herself, receiving him like a royal guest. Rocking in slow delight, another wave soon struck, she dug her well manicured nails deep into his back. "Get in bed my man, I want to serve you!" she cried. As he rolled over, her dress flew over her head as she climbed onto his chest. His hands clenched her round, firm tush guiding her to his mouth. As his mustache hit her, it vibrated through her. When that tongue entered, she couldn't resist. Riding and grinding as she never had imagined honey flowed from her like a river.

Falling to him, she felt him again, pressing at her, into her, fully inside her. So much more than she even desired, her mind raced as he fed on her breasts and probed her virgin tush. In her frenzy his cock slipped out and invaded her tush. She froze at the contact, took a deep breath, and began thrusting back. With squeals of delight she took every inch again and again until, as if commanded, they reached that final heavenly honor. They fell together, kissed and held tight, prolonging the genuine happiness and contentment of the moment.

They drifted off to sleep intertwined; they were able to ignore the insanity surrounding them. Peacefully, they both slept. As Sonia stirred she found herself holding her prize, "What has become of me?" she thought, as nature compelled her to stroke it to full size. In an effort to not wake him she turned her back to softly accept him. As she rocked to her first rolling orgasm she felt that strong hand on her hip, as she reached for it those fingers found her clit as his thrust slapped thick balls against her. "Lord, YES!" she cried, thrust after thrust sent her trembling. He rolled to his back and tossed her onto him, in a 69, something she had never experienced. The sensations he offered every bit of her loins as she gorged on him brought them to joint oral extravaganzas!

The sun began to break the horizon, Sonia rolled to find only a pillow. She was scanning the room and she saw Rick at the table working frantically. He turned to mouth silently "Get dressed and pack up Sugar." The sex and emotion was amazing but the high pace circumstances around her were just plain sexy! She sprang to her feet and inhaled the lingering scent of passion in the air. It was energizing in itself. He had put jeans, a blouse and sneakers out for her with her little .38 and a holster. As he worked silently, he helped her dress and conceal the pistol, she suddenly couldn't wait to learn how to really use it.

Once dressed, he signed off from the call, "Sugar pie, there was a bombing at the airport. We have a car waiting outside, we have to get on the road." She questioned nothing, gave him a warm good morning kiss and grabbed her things. They moved through the hotel smoothly but with the most deliberate actions. They were greeted by the Station Chief and an Agent, who advised Rick that there was a rifle with six magazines in the back seat. There was also a burner cell with 50,000 Euros in the glove box, and their route options to Rome. "Rome?" she thought, "What happened to London", Rick saw her expression "I will explain on the road, OK?" She nodded quietly.

And they were off, in a slick Alfa Romeo Coupe, sexy and quick, and handled like a dream. "Where are the ejection seat and machine gun switches?" she giggled. Rick replied, "USA, not 007 baby doll but we are on another adventure. Life with you isn't boring at all. The airport sustained major damage from firebombs last night. The new British PM heard about what happened here yesterday and panicked. He actually took actions to *advance* the Socialist agendas. The new Italian leadership put in a request for us, actually. But this arrival is low profile, here is your new passport, Mrs. Rose Gionfriddo. You are now the wife of Giuseppe Gionfriddo, welcome to your next Honeymoon."

"A girl could get used to these exciting Honeymoons, I wonder what a real one would be like?" She asked, looking over the maps. She saw mostly back roads through Switzerland, Austria and into Italy. "Are we allowed stops?" She asked.

"Well, the back seat has a cooler with deli meats, cheese, fruit, and veggies. There are also pastries, bread and drinks. We will be stopping for gas and restroom breaks. We have a great villa in Pordenone tonight, I think you will love it. Everything in that town is just gorgeous." Rick was so focused, a million "what ifs" ran through his head, as he checked every car or pedestrian for the next attack.

Sonia was so taken by the beauty of the countryside once they were out of the city, then into the mountains. In all of her European trips she had never seen this side of the continent, it was a living work of art. To every man's desire, she dug into the fixings in the back seat. Rick didn't complain about the view of her amazing bumm in the air filling his 'rear view mirror". He couldn't help but laugh out loud. "What?" she said. "Everything is great" he replied, as he gave her a swift swat on her round cheek. Her giggle was followed by a swish of her hips.

She returned to her seat, prepared to share, salami, cheese, olives, tomatoes, bread, and sparkling water. Sonia's gentle fingers placed each bite into his mouth. Then some pastry and a thermos of espresso. What a lunch! As they made their way down a deserted country road, Sonia said nothing as she put her head on his chest and hand on his waist. She began to nibble on his neck and she opened his pants, out it sprang and she squeezed it like a handle.

Not a word was spoken as she began to kiss, lick and suck with such incredible skill. She worked to make it last, without warning she accelerated her pace and intensity until…Ohhhh that hot steaming delicacy, "Yum" was her one word as she returned for every drop from him! Reluctantly she put him back together, knowing they were stopping soon. She patted his package as she buttoned him up. "I need some wine!" she said, and that butt was back in the air. She returned to her seat and sipped on a glass of Merlot. She offered him a sip before they came to a stop.

"Guten Tag, Benzine, Bitte," he said."Really…" she thought as he continued to speak with the Austrian Gas Attendant. He topped off, making her wait until he was done before running to the WC. Once he parked, off they went to take care of themselves. To her surprise, he went in with her. Not happy, she went along with it. But when he made her come with him, she wondered, "What is he not telling me?" Once on the road again she had to know, "OK, level with me, what is really going on?"

"You deserve to know, we have many enemies within, Italy is our safest bet. They are the only country standing strong, even leaders back home are mad at us for yesterday. No Balls! They sent us out to do this but then they won't support us. We are going to lay low for a bit. I have family in Sicily and we can stay there as long as needed, we will be very safe!" Rick reached for her hand to reassure her.

Down the winding roads they went, Sonia curled up on his shoulder more content than she ever had been in her life. She had the utmost confidence in her safety and in her man, and he was *her* man!

CHAPTER 5

As they entered Italy she had no idea what it meant to be Mrs. Gionfriddo, or Ms Bianci for that matter. She was not raised as a traditional Italian and knew very little of her family history. As they approached their stop Sonia began reviewing information on the small Northern community. The history is rich and embedded in the residents, what an honor it is to be welcomed in such a storied place. On the outskirts, they came to a beautiful home on a hill, not large but amazing nonetheless. It was surrounded by grape vines on one side and olive trees on the other, "Wow" had never said so much.

At the door was a bellissimo young woman in a peasant dress. "Buona sera Signore

Gionfriddo!" They entered the home and she gave Sonia a hug and kiss on each cheek, "Piacere". She said to Rick with approval. Lucia,the lovely lady of the house,assisted with everything from the car and directed Rick to a package that arrived from "Carrado", which was the proper code word. Once in the bedroom, he opened it, revealing several additional items such as suppressors, more ammo and money. There was also a set of Argentine Passports for them, these were not encouraging. Rick went out to the olive grove with the burner cell, Sonia had no idea what was happening but saw the items and knew it wasn't good.

Rick returned smiling, in Italian he loudly proclaimed "My love we are going to stay here for the next month, no one and nothing to bother us. We can enjoy our tranquility with Lucia and the countryside." In English he whispered, "We have a meeting in the morning, we will say we are going for a picnic but we are heading to Sicily. My family has everything set."

They enjoyed dinner, a warm bath and some much needed rest. As much as Rick could not relax, Sonia slept soundly. He woke her in the morning with a carnal attack that rivaled a dream. She screamed in delight. When she saw Lucia sneaking a peak she became even more motivated and took all she could get!....

As they prepared for the day she inquired, "Was that for me or a show?" "All for you my dear, but I am glad Lucia will report that we are madly in love! Now we need to get moving, can you distract her so I can get loaded up?"

"Oh yes, I am going to tell her of our exploits and have her knees shaking!" Sonia laughed with an evil note. Sonia went to the kitchen, where Lucia greeted her with a steaming coffee. The ladies sat making small talk. Lucia commented on what an amazing couple they were and said she wished she could find a man like Rick. Sonia began talking of their fiery romance, as she became descriptive Lucia's face was flushed and her nipples stiffened. Sonia gave in to the power of the moments, becoming more graphic in her descriptions of his cock in her mouth, bursting down her throat. Lucia began sucking a biscotti and pinching a nipple through her thin linen top. Sonia squeezed her knees tightly as they rubbed together, all but forgetting that Rick was secreting their escape. Stirring her coffee with her finger was the best way to keep it engaged. As Sonia went into how she loved the way he took her, stuffing her tight walls and trembling tush, Lucia pulled up her skirt to touch her bare, wet lips. In seconds she was shaking with a foot up on the table. Sonia was about to join her when the women heard him coming into the room. He closed to kiss Sonia, and she reached for his zipper pulling his pants off.

That fat cock sprang to life, Lucia sat watching silently as Sonia worked her magical mouth. After a few swallows he pulled her to her feet and bent her over the table, flipped up her little dress and he took her from behind. From tip to base with every deep thrust his fat balls slapping her clit, he reached to free her tits to bounce. Lucia said nothing as she freed her tits, climbing on to the table to match her own motions with theirs, stroke for stroke. In moments the ladies were grunting as they gushed, he pulled from her to tease her, running his tool through the cleavage of Sonia's ass.

Lucia quickly shifted position to swallow it, in seconds it was shooting in her throat. Still silent she took her full mouth to Sonia's and they exchanged a soft very wet kiss. As Rick recovered, he reminded Sonia, "We really have to get going."

As Sonia put herself together Lucia whimpered "Will I get more?" They both smiled and nodded as they made their way to the door.

They hopped in the car and off they went, rolling down the road Sonia couldn't contain herself. She gushed. "That was so hot, I had no idea, it isn't like I want to have sex with a woman or share you but the energy was so incredible. To see this young woman want my man as much as I do only fuels my desire for you, never let me go!"

"I never would have expected this, my work has been my life but you are rapidly taking over. I have to keep my head, this could get hairy before we get to Sicily," he admitted. After an hour they pulled off behind a deserted barn. Moments later a car just like theirs pulled in with a man and woman in it, they exited approaching Rick. Words were exchanged just before he drew that pistol, shooting both of them in the head instantly. He returned to the car, "We have to switch cars, get our stuff, they were the enemy. As they moved the last items to the other car he began moving the bodies to their car.

Another car occupied by two women rolled in slowly, "Joey, nice ass!" they exclaimed in unison. "I am so happy to see you, we have a leak as you can see," he responded.

They both grimaced, shaking their heads, "We will clean this, are you taking our car or theirs?" "I am taking theirs, I took his hat and jacket. Sonia, put your hair up like hers, this may be a good break. Andiamo!" he conceded.

They were off yet again, Sonia was silent. When she did speak, she chose her words well. "Is this for real, a secret agent with Mafia connections, and now we are 'On the lamb?'" Rick replied, "If you have to put it that way, yes. But we never use that word, it's 'Family business'. Especially at 'Casa Cicce', as you will see. Life as a princess is about to begin, just roll with it 'Mia Ragatza.' Oh I know you watch what you eat, but indulge a little or it will be an insult. Wine will flow freely, just take it easy until you find your groove." He couldn't sugar coat it any further.

"Will there be a place for you to teach me to shoot and handle myself like you?" she begged. "We will have to do it in private, that is frowned on overall. Affection though is expected, don't be a doormat but, my glass should be full unless I say no. You should be at my side unless I have business to tend to, at the meals you fix my plate for me." He coached.

"I grew up like that and I have secretly longed for this, just men today don't like it and women think of it as weak. You do know that I am falling for you, head over heels!" She confessed. "Ti amo, mi amore." he replied. Without a word, she climbed onto him, with the biggest kiss, which nearly caused him to wreck!

As they neared the coast he received a message on the burner, "read it please" he requested. "Really, OK. Cena e Milo's, 20:00. Messina. Um, can you fill me in?" She said, confused.

"Ha, this one is easy. Dinner at Milo's, in Messina at 8:00. We are right on time". Before they knew it they were pulling up to the ferry, as he pulled on the attendant waived "Eh Ricco!!" Rick waved and raised a finger to his lips, the attendant lowered his head "Scuse!"

They exited the car, moving to the coffee stand for a fresh drink and a pastry as the sun was approaching the horizon. As Sonia nibbled the sweet, she looked deeply into his eyes and asked, "How long can we stay here?" With a huge smile, he responded "It depends on the wedding. As long as there is one, then, indefinitely"

"What? Are you? I mean, well I never, how......." she stumbled. "Our papers have us married and citizens, I actually am a citizen, and if you really want to stay, the family will demand a real wedding. Real names, real jobs, real home, but that is for you to decide" he said, as he held her hand and slipped a ring on her finger.

Sonia melted, floored and ecstatic at once, joining in the most passionate of kisses as her hands roamed his chest like it was fine silk. "Ti amo" she whispered, as the announcement of shore interrupted. He took her hand and escorted her back to the car, opening the door and guiding her in. She had never had a man treat her this way and in a matter of days she knew she would never want to be without it.

As they approached the gate, two young men, visibly armed, opened the gate waving them in. "Is this Milo's?" She quietly asked, almost sheepish. "No, we are home. Milo is my cousin, his place is on the other side of the hill. Relax, this is easy!" he reassured her. As the car entered a courtyard, family members of all ages came out waving. When the car stopped, her door was opened by an older gentleman, Rick opened his door to the open arms of an older woman who was beaming.

They exited to hugs, kisses and so much being said. Sonia could make out some of it, mostly how happy they are to see him and for him to be with her. As they entered, Rick went out back with the men Sonia was ushered into the kitchen with the women. This was an experience completely new to her. They sat her down. The eldest spoke first, "What are your intentions? Are you after money or his heart? Are you committed to him or are you just another American thief?" They all stared. Sonia began, "I understand your concerns, Ricardo is a man like I have never met before. He fills my mind, body and heart, while making me feel safe and loved!"

The youngest spoke, "Can you do the cooking in the kitchen and the bedroom?" "He loves the way I feed him and what I feed him. As for the bedroom, It isn't only in the bedroom. I give him all he wants and everything I think he may want, he fuels my desires." she responded with confidence. "Hmmmm, we will see, andiamo," they said, as they led her out to the back to the men.

Meeting with the men, the women all pair with their man. Sonia was no different, offering a warm kiss as she melted to his side. They walked down a dimly lit path to Milo's and truly relaxed for the first time since she met him!

As they got to Milo's she followed the other women getting drinks for their men and moving to the kitchen. There, the women began presenting the first and second course. Salads, cold cuts, cheeses, "Wow! I could get huge…" she thought. As they all nibbled, came the veal, fresh bread and so much more. She remembered all he had said and saw how the women cared for their men and how the men swooned over the women in return. It all made so much sense, it actually was turning her on! As they savored the dessert, she thought of the relaxed night ahead for them. When the time came to pick up, she rushed to get things completed. When she returned to his side as he sipped Sambuca, "We need to get to our room," she whispered.

As they approached the villa, she was taken by its romantic beauty. The ladies had been there, lit candles as the door opened, a small fire in the stove and oh, what scents. As they approached the bed, she stopped him, saying "I want you to know exactly how I feel about you." She kissed him warmly over his mouth, chin, neck and ears as she unbuttoned his shirt. When the shirt hit the floor her hands moved over his chest and belly, and her lips did too, as she released his pants to the floor.

It was right there at eye level as she guided him to the bed to remove his shoes as she gazed up into his eyes. With him stretched on the bed, she slowly removed her sweater and light dress. Walking to him in the candle light, her beauty was staggering, the movement of her delicate delights were driving him wild in anticipation. She crawled from the floor of the bed, letting her breasts, legs and hair lightly glide over his skin until her lips met his again. Sliding up, she fed him her breasts as his hand found her boiling coochie, shuddering as he stroked the lips and clit. Needing so much more, she rose to lower her burning need to his mouth. In a frenzy, he went to work with his mouth as waves washed over her in ways totally foreign to her. Sliding down she found his cock, sinking it fully as it stretched her. Slow deliberate passion consumed them as the clock ceased to exist. In their rapture, they drifted off, entangled as one until the morning.

When he woke, she was laying on his chest looking over him, before he could speak her lips were on his. Without a word he rolled her to her back, her thighs already drenched, she accepted him with no resistance. With the greatest of sensations he tended to their carnal needs. As the reality of the day kicked in, they got up to take a quick shower and meet the family for breakfast.

This was a new experience for her, an egg on a piece of bread with a slice of prosciutto, some fruit and juice. It is so different, the men and women paired up in every way. The men quietly talked of business as the ladies prepared them for the day. When they had finished eating, the men ushered Rick out with them. The ladies took Sonia into their circle, they had planned a day in the town.

Before she could say a word, she was in a large sedan with the 'Madonna' who seemed to be grooming her into a baptism by fire. As she made herself comfortable, the driver handed a sweet orange drink to the ladies before leaving. They arrived and the market area bustled with activity, many waving at the large auto. As they parked, several residents approached the doors to open them and greet the women. They began viewing the items for sale, from fresh fruit to hand made shoes. As she inspected a handbag, the shop owner inquired if she was Rick's beautiful young wife. When she responded "Si", he took the bag, wrapped it, and wished her a happy marriage as he handed it to her. "How is it that they know her as family already?" she wondered.

When they paused for coffee, the barista addressed every lady by name including Sonia. He knew how each of them liked their drink, what cookie to pair with it. Sonia was impressed and in awe. No money ever changed hands, just smiles. "How is this?" she wondered, then asked aloud of Carmen (the youngest wife) "How is it that we don't pay for anything? that feels wrong." With a giggle Carmen schooled her, "Our men and joint investments make every business here prosper. We fund loans, help with family emergencies, promote their advertisement and so much more. We ensure there is no crime either, see our men at every corner? No one would dare to steal from them. We love our community and they love us. Our family has conducted this business here for over a Century. You are part of us now and forever!"

A perspective never imagined was coming into focus, everyone working to do their part happily. They moved to the hair salon, every seat was empty with a glass of wine waiting at each one. As they entered and the door was closed. A man remained outside. The ladies moved to a small room in the rear where they removed their dresses and donned soft linen robes. As they changed, she realized the others had no panties on, most didn't wear a bra either. "Hmmmmm, this is making so much sense" she thought.

Moving to the sinks, they each had their hair washed with the greatest of care. Such pampering! As her hair was washed, she realized her feet were being washed and dried before being placed in slippers. She received a nice hair cut, like she had never experienced. When they began to dress again a sweet girl presented her with a new dress and a pair of lovely shoes. "Where are my things?" she thought, Carmen noticed her concerned expression "everything is being sent home, worry about nothing."

Before they had time to think, they were at an amazing restaurant, where the men were waiting, already drinking wine. The ladies paired off, as always, to join their man. This is true history alive, as they all were greeted with warm kisses. They enjoyed a late lunch which they finished in time for siesta. Back to la casa.

Arriving they went to their villa, Sonia was astonished, this was new to her in so many ways. In their privacy she modeled her new hair, shoes, dress, and bag. As she did, Rick removed all but his pants. Moving to her, he used just one finger to begin removing her dress. It fell to reveal one breast and then the other, her fat nipples were rocks. When she let the light linen dress fall it revealed a silky freshly waxed prize, still pink and slightly swollen. Oh so sensitive he thought as he guided her to the edge of the bed and took a knee. His mustache and lips began gliding up and down her legs, around her lips, teasing her clit and tush.

As she reached for him, he flipped her legs up and wide, making her fall to her back as those amazing breasts bounced. The view made her that much hotter, "Oh please!" she cooed. The tongue assault began intensely, stuffing into her dripping pink as his bristling whiskers drove her clit insane. Her own anticipation put her over the top as his chin ground into her slick tush too. Her legs clamping to his head encouraged him to gorge that much more to keep the waves crashing over her.

After bucks and squeals of delight overwhelmed her, he rose to offer his twitching tool as it bounced on her drenched, dripping lips. With one thrust he invaded her, forcing honey to squirt over her hips. Long deep thrusts impaled her vigorously until she squeezed him out. Steaming nectar squirted from her, covering them. She crawled to her knees. What a sight she was as he pressed on her. With a buck she took in the head. Rocking back and forth she took every inch to her delight. A swat on her round ass distracted her as she felt a thumb enter her tight bumm, "Oh yes" she grabbed his wrist and stuffed his thumb into the base. In a whirling torrent she burst again, falling from him.

Flipping around again she opened her mouth wide to savor that bulging cock, as she swallowed he fondled her aching nipples. With a deep suck he gave her the boiling shots she hungered for. She devoured every drop before he curled up with her to drift off to sleep.

CHAPTER 6

An hour later they heard a knock and the door opened. An attractive middle aged woman announced she was there to clean. To Rick's surprise, Sonia told her to enter, seeing them she attempted to excuse herself. Sonia said "No, stay. Please do your work." She introduced herself as Isabelle as she attempted to begin cleaning, as she worked Sonia gently massaged and kissed him.

He couldn't resist the swelling in the moment, with a grin Sonia shifted her attention to it and his fat balls. Slow strokes, kisses and licks, which Isabelle tried to ignore. But Sonia's noises of approval made it impossible. Torturing Isabelle, Sonia climbed onto his hungry mouth, sliding her clit on his chin. He could no longer see and he wondered what could be happening. As Sonia neared satisfaction, he heard what he believed was Isabelle, moaning in excitement. Sonia trembled as she drowned him in honey, only to slide down and take it all in one smooth movement. With Sonia leaning back Isabelle began kissing and touching her body, sending her into a whole new perspective of bliss.

In moments Sonia fell to her back as Isabelle was guiding him to her waiting bumm, as he entered, she bucked down to accept it in joy. With

Isabelle's mouth working feverishly on Sonia's most delicate skin a joint explosion ensued. Volumes of juices flowing over them, which Isabelle devoured, while still bringing herself to a final release. Sonia fell to Rick, smothering him in kisses as Isabelle slid her body over theirs to join in the kissing.

Sonia whispered, "I have never, but I can only imagine....." Isabelle stumbled, "the beauty of you two consumes me to do things I would never... What do we...." Rick lavished in the affection of these beauties, ensuring he remained focused on Sonia as Isabelle fed them her full breasts and hard nipples. The view of them sharing her fueled their desires compelling Sonia to turn into a 69 position.

As Sonia kept him occupied, Isabelle climbed over him to rub her clit on his fat balls and the base of his cock while Sonia worked it to a rigid frenzy again. As Isabelle trembled in pleasure, Sonia mounted him once again. The two women sharing the sensations of lust consumed the entire room, their bodies rubbing and colliding as they worked to a symbiotic wave of release like none of them had ever imagined. Crumbling in delight they basqued in their glow and enjoyed the bliss that never was conceived before.

A jingle on Isabelle's phone reminded her of the time, in a rush she dressed, "So sorry I must go!" As she dressed Sonia grinned widely, "Will we see you again?" She smiled and nodded excited as she ran out the door. "Honey, is it bad how incredible that was?" Rick simply kissed her with the greatest of passion. They remained conjoined with total contentment.

Things were the quietest they had ever been in both of their lives. The fear that had filled her was replaced with passion, she found a *real* man who was "for her" and for the first time in her life she was "for her man". As he slept she petted his hairy chest, twirling it in her fingers. She had found hair on a man repulsive until now, she never hungered for sexual excitement like this either.

The chiming of her phone surprised her, as it had been silent for days, Harvard? Reading the message surprised her even more, an offer of a permanent position as a professor, "Why now?" she asked herself. Reading on, it continued that her expertise was a critical resource to building the minds and influence of their students and faculty.

Years, hell, days ago she would have accepted immediately, now I need to ask Rick. Would it really be worth leaving this life?

Rick's phone began buzzing and flashing, an "ASAP" display. Completely out of character she answered it so he could sleep. "Hello, this is Mrs. Gionfriddo, can I help you?"

"Hi, is Joe there?" a man asked in English. "He is busy, how can I help you?" she asked confidently. "Please have him call Tommy, you folks need to arrange a honeymoon home now." and the call ended.

Hearing the conversation, Rick stirred, she responded with a kiss and caresses.

"Tommy called," she whispered. "Do you want to be one forever, seriously?" he asked. "We can get married tomorrow, Mrs. Sonia Cicce?" A deep long kiss answered, "Only if we can come back here to stay after we finish this mission."

He grabbed the phone, "Mamma, Domani Preggo, Tutti Familia! Sie, tu Padre, 1400, Bene, Grazie! Ciao. It is done, mamma will have everything set for 2:00 tomorrow afternoon. Everyone is ready, you need to get to the house to get your dress ready."

"But, how, already? You had this all planned?" he simply smiled wide. She jumped and ran to the shower. Giggling, she ran, bouncing her gorgeous body as she dried and dressed. She jumped into her shoes, gave him a quick kiss, "Ti amo!" she cried as she ran out the door.

Rick grabbed the phone to finalize plans for the wedding. Then arranged a flight to Boston in two days. He thought, "This is the real challenge in the homeland. How do we get one of the most liberal danger areas to see the light over money?" Just then, a crypto message came in, "keep her under eyes coming home the old relatives are grumpy" it said.

He knew the real meaning for this, the invite to Harvard was a way to bring her in and make an attempt on her life and martyr her as a hero of their cause. With the wedding tomorrow, it will force leadership to work with him to plan this. He started with travel and lodging plans, with arrival in Boston two days away. With a non-stop from Rome to Logan he would have the best control and keep access to her limited.

The agency would be providing a car and driver. They would be staying in a safe house outside of the city and be returning to Italy two days later.

While he planned behind the scenes, Sonia was with Mamma Rosa and Carmela finalizing the church, meal plans, music and arrangement of decorations. As they came to agreements there was an announcement of the 'Dresses!' A group of ladies similar in size to Sonia appeared, wearing different options for her and the ladies of the wedding.

Rosa and Sonia focused on her dress while Carmela reviewed the others. The options ranged from simple to extravagant. Then there was a classic silk and lace simplified dress with a traditional veil. "This is one, isn't it?!" Sonia beamed. Not another word as Rosa escorted her and the model to a back room.

The model carefully removed the dress and donned a robe she had been provided. Sonia ignored everything as the ladies helped her into the gown that fit like a glove. It wrapped her amazing figure like she had been the perfect pattern for it. Turning to see her reflection it became real, she was a gorgeous bride for 'The man of her life'. Nodding and glowing they removed the dress like it was made of paper, as it dropped she couldn't hide her excitement, displayed by her rock hard nipples and shine trickling down her leg. The model smiled up at her as she admired the view, but Rosa's return to the room broke the moment.

"Hurry ladies, so much to do! I knew this would work perfectly, the chef is in the kitchen. Andiamo", Rosa commanded. Sonia got back into her own dress as the model rushed off, the heavenly scents were filling the house. As she entered the kitchen, trays of tasty delights awaited, from meat and cheese to pastry and cakes being fed to her like she was royalty. They began offering tastes in the order they would be served as she made her selections.

Then the cake, so many choices but the simple classic Cannoli cake of her childhood was the winner from the start! Still savoring the fabulous offerings, a parade of flowers began next. The aroma of roses and so much more offsetting the scents of culinary pleasure. Wading through the beauty, the simple came to the top like cream on milk.

Swimming in the florist presentation she couldn't resist gliding petals over her silky skin, ignoring the others present. She had never felt like such a lady, the feminist teachings were falling off as she began to realize the real power within her. Being a strong woman was so much more when she embraced being a woman, everyone and everything surrounding her made it a reality. Things wrapped up. It was time to get to the church, the Padre was waiting.

They arrived, noticing several other cars, but their driver seemed unphased, indicating the "family colleagues" were there. As they entered the church a few of the men greeted them while the others seemed to be examining the entire premise. They entered a door off of the altar, and she considered that she had never been granted access to such entry in her life. As she approached the desk, the priest rose to his feet and Rick appeared from behind a screen.

The ladies were met with comfortable chairs and warm tea, Rick took his place next to Sonia as a powerful older man sat with Sonia. The introductions began with the new figure, "Io Vito, Ricardo's Zio." "My late father's brother, he would like to give you away." Rick whispered. "Piaccera, Si! Preggo, mia Zio too!" she bubbled. Vito smiled and sat more upright, if that was possible.

As the priest ran down the plans for the next day, the discussion began about the service details. Sonia kindly interrupted, "Would everyone be comfortable with a true traditional service with old world vows to honor, cherish and obey?" The room went silent as huge smiles grew, Rick held and kissed her, Rosa squeezed her hand in reassurance. "So it will be." Father Luca concluded. A toast of Limoncello was passed as they concluded.

The day was shifting to dinner, as they traveled to Uncle Vito's Rick asked, "What about your parents?" "Mom passed away when I was 30, dad has been distant but I think he would love to be here." "Let's call him then," Rick said, as he pulled out the phone. Sonia dialed slowly, "What do I say?" she thought.

"Daddy, it is Sonia, how are you?" her lip quivering. "It has been so long, I miss you. I need to tell you something and ask you something. I am getting married tomorrow in Sicily, can you get on a plane tonight if I arrange it? You would! Oh!! I love you, I have been so wrong but I see the light now." As she sobbed, Rick took the phone, introducing himself. He advised Carlo (he was known now as Carl) that a plane would be at his local airport at 5:00 that afternoon, he just needed to bring a passport and a suit. "Yes sir, Yes sir, me too, I have resources, see you in the morning!"

She was beginning to stop asking how he does things, or what he is doing when she isn't around, she just loved it! She knew he had 'family business', he works for the "Agency", but which one? He has means, but from where? Not knowing what this meant for her didn't matter, she felt secure, included and truly happy for the first time since being a little girl.

Arriving at the family home Sonia was ushered to the kitchen by the ladies. Now it was time to cook. She was invited to be in the kitchen for the first time, all of the other women knew their places and got to it. Carmela, being the youngest, took Sonia by the hand, "Be my helper, I will teach you how this works!" Sonia followed her direction as they worked like a well oiled machine. They were making the bread first, then on to pasta. Another lady was on sauce, while another worked meats, another did cheeses. Mamma Rosa did dessert, an amazing olive oil cake with what was going to be a mascarpone topping. So simple and amazing, Rosa worked diligently while supervising the rest of them, occasionally giving direction.

They all sang Italian love songs as they worked, the atmosphere was fulfilling and exciting at the same time. These women did this out of love and devotion and not as a chore! The songs were new to her but said everything she was thinking and felt. This was a life she never knew and never thought she could love. At 45, Sonia never had children. Her family wasn't close and in her profession, personal relationships never went this way. However she thought, she never *let* it go this way either, Rick was the kind of guy she never would have given a second thought to.

As the meal began to come together Carmela and Stella took her off to another room, where a huge copper tub was filling with hot water and bubbles. A vanity table was set up with a pretty little silk dress hanging over a chair. "Now we get you ready for tonight!" Stella exclaimed. Soft music played as she got into the tub, the water was perfect with rose petals floating around her. Carmela washed her hair as Stella shaved her silky legs, what an experience.

Soon it was time to rinse and dry. Wrapped in a towel, they did her hair and nails as she sipped a sweet orange liquor. Before she knew it the girls had to get ready themselves, "We will be back in 20 minutes to help with the dress and escort you out, don't mess up your hair but relax."

Sonia tried but relaxation was not in her tonight, "Wow" said volumes. In a flash they were back dressing her, it was already 18:00 (6:00 pm) the day had flown by. Standing before the mirror she was delighted with what they had done for her. Now-to her man! As the three walked to the great family table, soft music played while laughter and banter could be heard. They crossed the threshold and silence fell, even the children stopped to appreciate Sonia entering the room. Rick went to her side, taking her hand to escort her to their seat.

Pausing he announced, "My family, my lovely bride! Please welcome her into our fold as one!" Cheers followed, as they rose to their feet raising glasses "Salute". She blushed, thanking them, then stopped to kiss him for all to see! As dinner rolled through she couldn't resist slipping off a shoe from time to time just to run her toes up and down his leg.

Finishing dessert and cafe she whispered, "Honey, I have your dessert ready, we should go." Without a word he stood and waved as he took her hand and off they went with laughter following them. As they approached the villa she stopped him, "I never knew I could feel this way!" Without a word he scooped her up, carrying her as she clung to his neck kissing around his face.

Inside, he stood her at the bed, dropping her dress to the floor. She began slowly undressing him, dancing as she did so. After removing his shoes and socks and pants, she gazed up at him, kissing the tip and down the length then tracing it with her tongue. Cool as ice but boiling inside he pulled her to her feet, kissing her deeply as he laid her on the bed. She welcomed the pressure below and accepted him completely. Like classical music they rocked with perfect rhythm, only to be interrupted by his need to savor her steaming honey.

What felt like hours passed as they shifted in true passion until they drifted to sleep. Morning came with him poking her tush, without a word she accepted the morning bliss until once again she was a puddle of happiness. After warm intense kisses he was off to the shower to take care of things and then vanish until the wedding. She watched as he dried, shaved and dressed. Her mind was filled with thoughts of the years to come and the joy it will bring along the way. With a kiss he was gone, she drifted back to sleep with the best thoughts she could imagine.

CHAPTER 7

As the sun cracked through the window Sonia was awake, fixing the caffe. She settled in to lounge in her silk robe, when there was a knock. "Sonia, andiamo di Sposare!" The ladies were there already! "What was really in store for the day?" she thought as the door opened. They hurried her out to the main house to the same room where she was prepared yesterday. Another hot bath was running, her dress stood on a form, and an army of family ladies bustling about. Rushing around her needs, the ladies worked to get themselves ready too. Over the next several hours they blossomed into a team of gorgeous. Time flew by, and suddenly, it was off to the church!

Arriving, she was greeted by church staff, family friends, and the Security Team. Upon crossing the threshold, she froze. "Oh Papa! Ti amo!" wrapping her arms around her father in joy. She had been so distracted by the preparations, she had forgotten to prepare herself emotionally for their reunion. "No crying", he said "you will ruin your make up my child, so beautiful on such a "belle oggi! Vito and I have decided to give you away together as one familia, now off you go mia figlia". He directed her with a smile and kiss.

Off she went for final prep, the sounds of guests and the music filled her heart. In what seemed like a flash, her veil was on and a knock at the door. This was suddenly *very* real. Vito and her father stood there in their black suits with huge smiles and outstretched hands. Without hesitation she offered her arms, which they took gently and guided her to the aisle.

As the music started for her last walk as a single woman, she knew it was not a dream, although it felt like one.. She took in the sight of the altar, the ladies and men waiting, but did not see Rick. As she approached, the priest and her beloved walked out of the vestibule. She beamed, and from the second she took his waiting hand, time accelerated.

All too quickly, as if she had not been paying attention, the vows had been said. "I do!" rang out, and rings made it official. A month had just become a lifetime sealed with a steaming passionate kiss. The recessional walk down the aisle as Man and Wife filled her with excitement and desire! Getting into their ride, she kissed him with abandon, and pulled up her dress as they drove away. Not a word was said as she displayed her silky smooth, wet mound before freeing him. Climbing onto him, she exhaled with love; he filled her in all of the *best* ways. The screen gave her privacy but she didn't even care, she actually needed him. Releasing a full tit from her gown, she fed him as she consumed the most amazing cock, they rose to magnificent waves of mutual delight.

Pulling into the gates, she knew it was time to release him and reassemble themselves. They were just ready as the limo came to a stop. The driver had taken a long route so the family was able to arrive and organize for their arrival. As they exited, the party began. They played, and the music rang! The revelry was interrupted by the sound of shots fired and a blast in the distance. Vito and her father left with some of the other men. "Papa too?" she said to herself, feeling confused.

Rick took her hand and they returned to greeting their guests. She knew she was safer than ever before, especially knowing *real* men were facing the danger that had always surrounded her silently. With Vito and her father returning, the traditional events continued: the Father-Daughter dance, followed by the Mother-Son dance, and the cutting of the cake.

As the sun set they moved to the villa. With the greatest of romance their clothes fell to the floor, and they fell into each other. Waves of pleasure filled her and her loins were drenched, she savored each and every sensation that could be consumed in her vault, tush and mouth. Her entire being appreciated his every touch. He missed nothing, from her hair, to her nipples, all the way to her curling toes. Even in her rapture, she relished the views and electricity from his body.

They slept in spurts, waking each other throughout the night. They welcomed the interruptions as necessary, whether to satisfy their carnal needs or simply touch and appreciate the other's warmth. Morning came. He was awake first, she met him in the shower which had become such a sensual place for them. Without a word she dropped to her knees, kissing, licking, sucking, tasting the benefits of their honeymoon bliss. Still swollen, she needed more. She rose to her feet and turned to rub that fat toy through the cleavage of her bumm. His fat fuzzy sack tempted her clit with every motion, in the next shift that fat tip was pressing her lips.

Wet from within, her lips opened and welcomed him in one deep push. His hands on her hips and back, bouncing tits, down her belly to her trembling clit she was awash in desire. With a burst of lightning she pushed him out and gushed over him. Without hesitation in her shuddering state, he turned his attention to her delicate ass. She froze before thrusting back to take it. Using the wall, her arms pressed repeatedly to bring them to a final eruption!

Returning to a full embrace, they cleansed each other to prepare for the next journey. Within minutes, the traveling pros were dressed, packed and ready to move out. They moved into an SUV, flanked by the two escort vehicles. It was strangely real; something she never could have expected would come from her work. "Is this all for me?" she inquired.

"It is, but you are worth it, and we enjoy it. The guys have trained for this for decades, the peace we have maintained has made them a bit soft. The community is a huge help and we appreciate their safety. This has been knocking on the door for years in the shadows. Now off we go, your father is flying with us to Boston and he is leaving for home from there. We are in first class together, the family bond is strong!" She responded with a full embrace and consuming kisses.

Breakfast was packed for them. Slowly they savored the meal as they did each other. When they finished, the airport was in sight and it was time to transition back to public view. Exiting, they joined her father, who rode in one of the escort cars. His eyes were wide as Rick guided them through his diplomatic resources to the VIP gate.

The brief wait to board allowed for some family bonding. When it was time, they were the last to board, and had the front seats of first class. Rick and Carlo quickly were becoming friends, Carlo never had a son and Rick was everything he could have ever wanted in a son. They had the same views, similar upbringing and family values. Sonia had never understood this, embraced it, or realized how these aspects formed her life. It all began to make so much sense. For a woman who bends minds, it took her a while to get it! She was becoming so much more overnight, she is Mrs. Ricardo Cicce!

CHAPTER 8

They arrived in Boston, it was mid day. An escort was waiting, and within moments their luggage was delivered to them. Sonia and Carlo said their goodbyes as he was taken to his connecting flight. They were off, her head had found the "swivel" she had previously mocked. She understood, it wasn't paranoia, but true situational awareness. She appreciated it now. "When can I learn to really use this?" she asked, as she tapped the pistol on her thigh. Rick's thought was immediately to something else but quickly realized her actual desire, "Let's do some dry work for now, then we will do some live work when we get back home Sugar."

Pulling up to the modest secluded home, a smartly dressed Agent exited the home. She greeted them with a smile, advising it was and will remain secure for their stay. They quickly settled in, Rick knew the home completely from previous use. The Security Agent, Crystal, reminded them she would remain out of the way but would be there during the entire stay to ensure no infiltration. Knowing the next day would start early, Sonia began rehearsing and asked for some privacy.

Rick went with Crystal to discuss the systems of the house and examine the vehicle they would be using over the next couple of days. The hours seemed like minutes; suddenly she realized she needed dinner as the scents of Rick in the kitchen helped reawaken her to her bodily needs. Entering the room, a twinge of envy overcame her; Rick was in the kitchen and Crystal. She was seated at the table, with a leg on the chair and her skirt riding up her legs as she sipped wine. Was it Sonia's imagination or was Crystal looking at Rick with the same longing that she has? "He is pretty delicious, isn't he?" Sonia said, as scooted her bare feet across the floor to kiss Rick warmly and grabbed a handful of his butt.

Crystal giggled "You absolutely are a lucky girl, many of us have tried but the mission and rules always kept him out of reach, You are some kind of lady!" Rick kissed Sonia back, sliding his hand under her skirt to squeeze her bare ass, fueling the challenge of the ladies. "Now back to dinner. We have sauteed sausage, pasta with olive oil and garlic sauce, and yes, of course Tapioca Pudding. Now play nice, be friends!" he commanded as he handed Sonia a glass of wine. With a kiss she squeezed his cock before turning and rubbing her round tush against him like a cat.

As she walked away he gave her a swat prompting her to jump and giggle, bouncing hard nipples pressed against her silk blouse. Crystal smiled, "We all knew he was an amazing monster, but 'MMMMMM' you are a lucky lady!" Sonia sat at the table and replied, "There was never anything planned, things just *happened* when we were forced together. He uses my skills against me and I love every minute of it. Plus...... he gives me pleasure and security I have never imagined. He has an incredible family, and then, there is the cooking! I will have to work hard not to get fat!"

"Now Sonia, stop telling stories! You attacked me, I just got sucked into your web!" he responded. "That isn't all getting sucked, I'm sure," Crystal said as she licked her lips. "OK ladies, I hate to distract you but dinner is up" he advised, carrying over the first pan. The girls hustled to get the table set, putting him between them. Once seated and served, they savored the fresh meal. Sonia did have desert on her mind, rubbing her gentle toes along his legs up to his thigh. She knew how he loved this. Wanting to torture Crystal in the moment, she can't resist. He squirmed and she knew it was growing, "Can I have some cheese baby?" she asked, just to make him stand.

As he did, they couldn't ignore that bulge, he was clued in and teased back in return. Approaching Sonia he stopped to shift his hard cock, when he bent to serve her she traced the outline with her finger tip. "Let's finish dinner first my lady," he said, and he returned to his seat. "Humfffff, Yes sir!" joked Sonia, returning her focus to her meal.

Finishing their last bites the ladies began to collect dishes and move to the sink. As they washed, the ladies swayed to the soft Italian music, their pretty buns putting on quite a show. Having had enough of the show, Rick moved behind Sonia, pressing against her ass as he guided his hand to the bottom of her breasts. His lips hit her neck and she pushed back against him and with a little grind.

"Come with me!" he demanded, taking her hand and whisking her to the other room. He left the door open and Crystal could hear everything. Sonia fell hard onto the bed, saying "Oh please, don't stop! Suck it, Huuugh," Crystal knew he was feasting on her dripping treasure, she could only imagine the vision of her honey running over his chin as hers was running down her leg. She fell to the couch and pulled at her skirt and panties in a rush, finally dipping her fingers into throbbing self. Calming and stimulating all at once, in only seconds she was squealing in her own release. Her eyes opened, and she had full eye contact with Sonia. Observing Sonia, who was filled with him as she smiled and squeezed her rock nipples.

Crystal shifted and tore her panties to give Sonia a full view of her drenched delight as her fingers worked their magic. In near perfect timing the three came to a staggering climax, Crystal had never imagined this scenario, but had no complaint! They all separated and retired to shower. Rick was completely unaware of the ladies' connection.

As she bathed Crystal's mind ran over the view she had just seen. She dropped her clothes like rocks while admiring her beauty in the mirror, her nipples were still swollen, and pussy lips remained puffy. Her clit tingled with electricity. Every touch was exhilarating, she pulled at a nipple and stroked her clit. This quickly she moved on to one, then two fingers in while sucking her nipple. Thrusting her hips to her hand brought the wave, an errant finger tip probing her bumm brought the final gasp! Slumping into the shower under the boiling water she found her relaxation.

They all fell to bed, drifting off happily. The sun rose and he was up and prepping for the day, inspecting the car, searching every item they were bringing and checking the guns. The ladies said nothing as they sat sipping coffee watching him with the same admiration. They both knew better than to even try to help, this was *his* time. He handed them each their weapons for the day, then came to the timeline. He was all business like last night never happened. It was difficult to focus on the mission with both of them boiling inside! Rick chastised, "Focus ladies! This must run like a clock. Sonia, remember, *you* are the bait. The teams are ready from when we walk out of the door. Rear security for our return is huge tonight. We expect the hit to happen at a 'choke point', the vehicle is hardened but a blast is overwhelming in any ambush. When it hits you must be ready to hit the floor as I get at it! When we break contact it is a must that we remain cool and let the team run the rest as we make it out. Crystal, you will remain in full contact with the team. If the hit comes en route we will be heading straight to Devens to meet with the MARSOC Team and fly out, you must E&E at the same time. If the hit is at Harvard the local police Helicopter will ex-fill us to Devens. If there is no hit we will be coming back, an extra team will be perimeter security here. If we can intercept them the day will go as planned and we will return here for the night and fly out in the morning. What are your questions?" They had none. He was clear on every aspect.

"Nothing," said Sonia, Crystal echoed, "Me neither". Rick seemed content, saying "Get dressed ladies, we roll in 90 minutes." While they dressed he did one more round while making multiple calls. In short order it was time, the typical "Saddle up" wasn't needed today, "Rock on" ran through every head at the same instance. Crystal took up security, they got into the car and out they went.

Coming to the first intersection they passed a sedan that stopped seconds before, on the interstate an MSP chopper flew ahead. Suddenly a flurry of radio transmissions sounded, then a burst of black smoke about a mile ahead. Without a word Rick hit the median, to the shoulder at 140mph to the next exit. An MSP cruiser rolled in front of them, they got on his bumper and stuck like glue until they neared the outskirts of Harvard. Without another word normal driving returned. Sonia sipped water and dabbed her face "Wow!"she thought.

"Take a breath my love, they got the first wave, head on a swivel! Big smile and all business. Now go!" he said as the car came to a stop in front of the 200 year old hall. With a deep breath she waited as he opened the door, watching his eye contact with the team surrounding them. Taking his hand the stress went into him as if she poured it out, her confidence grew like he was injecting it into her simultaneously.

With everyone in place, it was on! She was tuned in, and as she left his side to take the stage she was welcomed with cheers from the liberal students. She began commending their activist efforts; she got into their heads when she began to speak of hard work, accomplishments and dedication to what is right within the law. She still held them as she addressed life, the beauty of how it is formed and the blessings of their lives. She encouraged them to take the lead in raising their children as they grow to the next generation. Silence grew, "You MUST prosper to spread your message for the years to come!" she continued. Cheers began in return, "YOU are the hope to save us as we continue, but HOW can you do that without understanding family and why we have order? YOU are the order!" Cheers rang louder, Sonia went on, "Raise families as leadership sets, with the proper guidelines. Encourage success and excellence!" They roared their approval, having no real idea that her directives were in opposition to their current views. Raise children, rather than escaping the duty to your cause. Children are the joy but also the responsibility, life is NOT an endless party without direction.

As she concluded the cheers continued. While lost in the frenzy of their excitement, the crowd had no idea how the wild hateful ideas of killing babies was being washed from their understanding. Success, leadership, and responsibility were taking hold and the idea of using the law to help ALL again and abandon the insanity of the decadent socialist ways. They chanted "We are the LEADERS!" as she exited the stage into Rick's waiting arms, "Well done, my love. Time to git, stay with me." He directed.

As they made their way through the students and team members they approached a suited woman Rick didn't recognize. Saying nothing he moved her behind him. He got two steps ahead then turned quickly. As the woman reached into her coat he clobbered her. She fell to the ground and the officers behind them collected her, examining her coat, they gave the bomb signal while carrying her. Rick turned and snatched Sonia off her feet, tossing her to safety in the waiting car.

Rick jumped in, and they sped off as she sat on the floor gazing up at him with full trust.

"It may get a bit hairy!" he said. Two MSP cruisers met them as they turned out of the gate. As they approached each intersection a Trooper would speed up and block it for them to pass safely. Once on the Interstate they hit the left lane with lights blazing, as they passed several cars a trooper was sure to make space. Suddenly a car darted from the right lane toward them, the rear trooper collided with the left front door of the vehicle instantly killing the driver. Moments later the stopped bomb signal was sent to Rick, he just chuckled and shook his head.

She had yet to catch her breath as they neared the safe house, Rick said, "We really should change directions, we have a 'rat in the wood pile'!" With that he took the next exit turning toward New Hampshire, "Portsmouth! The family is waiting. You can sit up now," and he reached for her hand. The radio exploded as he turned it off, he slowed approaching a rest area where he turned and parked next to an old Chevy pick up truck. A couple exited and DANG! They looked like them. There was an exchange of keys, "Familia Casa, dua oggi mi amici!" he said.

In the truck they drove at a normal pace into Portsmouth and directly to the harbor where a large boat was waiting. They climbed aboard and sped off to a cargo ship that was waiting off the coast. They boarded and the captain directed them to what appeared to be a cabin on the modest commercial vessel. They opened the door and Sonia was shocked yet again. What a room! It had a full bath and small kitchen, with a lovely bed. As the sun set she felt safe again on the whirlwind of this vortex. Rick drew her a warm bath and then went to work with encrypted messages. He told her nothing and she asked no questions. She was confident that whatever he did was right.

There was a knock at the door as she was exiting the tub. There appeared a young man with a cart, the top covered. Rick wheeled it in and she had to know, "Are you going to tell me?" He removed the cover revealing an unexpected meal of lobster, pasta, oysters, and shrimp. Wrapped in a towel she sat at the little table. Rick poured the wine and she prepared plates side by side. They settled in and indulged in the fabulously fresh meal, "You never need restaurants do you?" She asked. He smiled, nodding no, as he fed her an oyster.

Finishing dinner she asked, "Can I do something for you?" "Of course, what is it?" he replied. She ran warm water, beginning to undress him as she kissed along his nakedness.. Once he was fully "neked" for her she used a small wet soaped towel to wash him slowly with the most delicate,sensual touch. When she finished, she rinsed him in the same way, lastly toweling him dry. Moving toward the beckoning bed, her towel dropped. In the pale light she resembled a painting gliding to him. She showered him with kisses as she mounted him, riding slow sensual waves of desire until they fell together and dropped off to the deepest sleep.

The next morning came with her waking first for a change, she gazed at him as his eyes opened just before the sun cracked the horizon. With warm kisses the day launched, reality returned as Rick stopped the feast of kisses to advise her a plane would be meeting them in 45 minutes. Rather than be disappointed she beamed at him, "Ti amo!"

Dressing in fresh clothes they enjoyed a breakfast left at the door, making the most of the current situation. A knock interrupted the quiet, a voice behind the door advised "10 minutes! The bird is inbound." They collected the few items and guns they had and moved to the deck.

As they got to the launch area the plane was in sight. With military precision they boarded the small craft, moving to the plane as it came to rest bobbing on the waves. They tied off briefly to get into the idling plane. With a hand shake, they were off. True to form, as they settled in they found a basket of food, drinks and conversation items. Sonia finally got comfortable, the drone of the prop engines put her into a deep sleep.

The plan worked, they were crossing over Portugal to land and change planes. "This is a very cooperative country for family business without issue." Rick would later explain. As they touched down, the other plane was waiting, Rick woke her with warm kisses and a gentle touch.

"Really? I slept the whole way? Where are we?" she inquired. "Portugal Sugar, grab the basket please" Rick responded as he grabbed the bag of his tools. He met the Family Team who were pulling security as they moved planes. "This family was its own private army" she thought. She had no idea this was how anything in the *real* world worked. She had been able to live such a comfortable opinionated life for decades. Rather than being disappointed at her ignorance, she felt grateful to be finally conscious of how things actually happen. She loved the totality of it!

As they boarded the simple military style plane there was an overwhelming feeling of comfort to be 'going home!' Never before in her adult life had she enjoyed such a feeling. Buckling in, they began the final taxi of the day. As they returned to the air she was pleased to assemble a meal for her man, she loved taking care of him the best way she could, knowing he was the reason she was alive. She was warm in her heart like never before as she fed him each bite in the most sensual way, with fun banter between them.

When they finished he knew what he had been seeking had finally come to be in Sonia. The plane rumbled through the sky with her laying her head on his lap as he covered her in a soft blanket. Not a word was needed to know how they both felt, so much danger was finally out of the way again.

The time had come, they were on approach to land at the small airport near the family home. "Am I finally going to be relaxing again? I love you and this place, I never want to go back to my old life." This was a first to move beyond her ideals to face a practical reality toward authentic peace. They were headed back to Sicily and she couldn't be happier than she was now with '*Her* man!'

Vito and Rosa were on the plane waiting with great delight, "Ricardo! He has come home to the family!" Rick smiled, proclaiming,"Oh Si!! I have advised HQ that my retirement is effective immediately, I have some things to turn over but I am here to stay! I have a wife to love and protect. I have a family I have neglected for a country who has turned its back on us for the LAST time! The trust is gone, there is no doubt the enemy knew where we were at every turn for this one."

During the flight, discussions were had of what lay ahead for the newlyweds; they could now enjoy their freedom and future within the family. Sonia was speechless when she learned that Carlo had an open invitation as a true family member! It was all coming together!

On the ground they soon were, and off to the waiting vehicles. Their new lives were on the way. Now, to get the next phase started. Once at the villa Sonia started a hot bath while Rick began the encrypted messages to finalize his retirement. He also began his new mission as the Family Security Leader, especially necessary in light of current events. He was in contact with allied families to secure the entire area between Messina and Syracuse. Aspects of the families were even in contact with aspects of the police to jointly root out and identify communist and anarchist elements in the area. They were like minded, the Italian way of life had to be preserved with integrity, honor, morals, family and tradition.

Shifting gears, Rick admired her figure in the bubbles as he approached, "Sugar, I have some meetings. I will be back before dinner, I would like to have a quiet night alone. I am working on something I would like to show you tomorrow, please don't make any plans." She smiled, leaning her head back to accept his warm kiss and caress.

As he walked out, she felt pleased with her new station in life. The happiness filled her heart and body as one, her head swam with ideas for dinner and what tomorrow may bring. Ignoring her excitement she dialed Carmela, "Hey, can we go to the market? I need to get things for dinner and I need to talk. Fantastic. Yes, I will be at the main house in 20 minutes!" She dried in a flash, and jumped into a little skirt, lace bra, linen top, and delicate panties. "Where did these come from?" she thought, "he loves no panties, I haven't worn a pair in so long...forget it! Sliding on a pair of sandals she grabbed her bag and scarf.

Reaching the house she thought, "Crap! Money..." Opening her purse she found a roll of Euro that had just appeared,"Sigh, he is something!" she said to herself. Opening the door she found Carmela, Rosa and some area ladies sipping coffee and enjoying biscotti, "Buongiorno! Come stanno i miei amici?" Sonia inquired.

"Il tuo italiano é! buono! Now! Andiamo in città," Carmela bubbled. As they were driven into town she felt so at home, pulling into the market area the sounds and smells brought *such* relaxation. As they moved through the streets their escorts moved in front and behind them, almost invisible to them. The men were community members and were welcomed, as they were, with fruit, a bite of bread or cheese, a sip of wine as they selected the delights: cheese, salami, bread, olives, tomatoes, eggplant, fish, eggs, even a freshly killed chicken.

Collecting their components they headed back to the villa. Carmela helped guide Sonia through prep and proper seasoning of each, time had flown and the clock showed 15:00 already. That chicken had to get in the oven, the eggplant had to get in the pan, salad, fish, and more. "Oh crap!" she giggled, it was all just so wonderful! Everything was coming together. Carmela opened the wine and scooted out the door.

Moments later Rick came in like a breeze, her hands full, she shook her tush as a wave. He responded by taking a handful of it and kissing her neck, his other hand on her soft belly exposed by her little top. "Ti amo," he whispered as his hand slipped under her skirt while the other teased the bottom of her breasts. With a soft moan, she kept working as she bent forward filling his hand with a breast and offering her wet coochie to the other. Nibbling her ears and neck, those fingers went to work bringing her a long awaited wave of steaming honey running down her legs. As he slowly brought her back to earth he drew his dripping hand to his mouth, to his delight she turned to share a taste of her honey. "Dessert will be especially nice my love, " escaped her lips before kissing him fully. "Now sit, dinner is ready!" she directed.

He sat happily at the set table, she brought a chilled bottle of Pellegrino 'Acqua Frizzante' and poured. She placed the salad, fish and bread out for them, with a kiss on his cheek. Sitting together she served him as she ran her bare toes over his ankle. When they finished, she set the pasta and perfect chicken before him. "Did you have help?" he asked. "This is fantastic, you are learning so fast!" She smiled holding up two fingers in a pinching position as she kissed his forehead, offering him a view down her top.

The wonderful meal was finished and she motioned him toward a soft chair where she served him a Sambuca and fresh pastry. She quickly cleared the dishes, collecting another Sambuca and pastry for herself as she moved to sit in his lap. They enjoyed desert and each other's pleasure that was like nothing they had ever had. "Sugar, this is a dream come true. I have to admit that your assignment was not my first choice, but the good Lord made the right choices to get us together. My life has taken turns I never expected, bringing things to light, and shifting my future which is present now. I have put some things in motion, one is going to be very clear in the morning, the rest you will be learning day by day," he offered softly.

"I do love it here. I never would have picked to have you attached to me either, but knowing what I know now, you are the archangel I needed and *need* for the rest of my life. I love what I am learning and this life I never expected, I had become so embedded in what I was doing that I had lost sight. Now my eyes are completely open to what was and is wrong as well as to what is right that I *must* embrace! I will follow you, please just don't stop considering me as we go. And just a hint for tomorrow? Please......" she responded.

Warm kisses were the message for the next 30 minutes until he lifted her into his arms to place her in the large bed. Her clothes melted off with his touch, as she pulled at his with the occasional pause to remove another steel item from his person. Once he was presented for her attention she was an inferno that pulled him to her as a second meal. He worked methodically with her desire to bring her the most intense passion wherever his mouth and fingers went. In a sea of moist heat she could wait no more, seeing her chance she pulled him to her, plunging him into her like a harpoon. With possession, her legs wrapped and clinched, preventing any separation. In the frenzy of bucking and grinding they came to rolling climaxes that resulted in a mutual collapse before they drifted into the warmest sleep.

As morning came she woke with a full bladder, rushing to relieve herself, the pale light shone over her amazing figure. She was admiring her own beauty for the first time in 20 years, returning next to him she snuggled close and watched him breath. This was the first time he ever slept through her moving, he was relaxed and content, finally. In her appreciation she delicately kissed his chest and nipples as her fingers played in his chest hair. As one hand traced his cock it began to twitch and swell, one tender finger moved to slide up and down the thick center of it. Knotting her hair up, not to tickle him she replaced her finger with her tongue. "I don't want to wake him but… YES!" she thought.

Like a cat she climbed over him, and guided him into her waiting nest without touching any other part of him. With the greatest skill she worked from the tip, back and forth to the mid point. Building her excitement in silence she had to touch herself to finish her needs. Finishing her second shuddering moment, she fell taking all of him. Little did she know, he had been awake and ready to respond. Clutching her round ass he thrusted vigorously stretching her with every motion, not a discernible word escaped either of them until she squealed "God I love this man!" With that, she fell to him like a magnet to her being.

Shortly the sun was rising as was Rick, "My love we need a shower and have to get going." Not another word, they happily bathed each other and prepared, he dressed in the most casual clothes she had ever seen him in. "Is this OK?" she asked, holding up a little black and white dress, his simple grin and nod was all she needed.

Like a native she prepared a simple breakfast and tea for them, he preferred the light nature of tea in the morning. Small talk and happy banter ruled the morning as they ate and cleaned up. "Andiamo, we have an appointment!" he barked with a kiss and swat on her bumm. "I just love your ass! Hmmm it may need some attention later today!" She said nothing, just bent at the waist flipping up her dress to display the naked beauty of it before running out the door in front of him.

She jumped in the car like a kid going to Disney, and sat waiting like he was denying her something. As he got the car going she had to lean and bite his neck, "I'm ready now, kind sir". He drove a short distance around and over a hill where a large but modest older home stood surrounded by trucks, men and women. "What now? More big family? I love it but I want more us time, hmmmm…" she thought as her mind whirled.

Coming up the drive, he read her mind, saying "Never assume my dear, this was my great grandfather's. Now it is ours, the fruit trees, the pool, the barn, the home, all of it! The paint is being finished, the kitchen was done yesterday, and the furniture gets here this afternoon. I had started this when we E&E'd here the first trip, all of the family kicked in, I knew this was right since Miami."

She bounced from her seat like a 'Tigger', smothering him in tits as she kissed and clutched his head. "A house for me? I have only had apartments! Land, a pool, fresh fruit, oh God, how much?"

"I had the money set aside and we did it with family help, they can be tough but you will grow to love them," he said as he parked. Her door flew open and she ran like a child skipping to the front door. "Well, come on you have to see it with me!" she called. As she reached the door Rosa and Vito greeted her with a basket containing the traditional housewarming gifts of wine, bread, and salt. As they spoke Sonia, was speechless, she wasn't ignoring but was completely distracted.

Rosa took her by the arm, guiding her through the lovely interior, the modest living room, large dining area, and grand kitchen with new appliances that looked 50 years old! "How did he know??? He does have ways…" she thought. A guest room was divided from another room by a large but simple bathroom. It was the next room that caught her off guard. The room was prepared, and perfectly, for a little girl. Rosa explained that this had been Ricardo's grandmother's room and now it shall be Gina's room. Sonia was totally lost, she asked "Um Gina? I need some help on this one, are we having a child that I am not aware of?"

"Grazie Zia Rosa! My dear, Gina is my cousin's daughter. My cousin's husband was killed by the anarchists two months ago and my cousin just died of cancer in the last two weeks, leaving Gina an orphan. Gina has been living with my Aunt Lucille, but she is very old. These women have conspired, they thought 'Well, Gina *is* only four' She is still a baby really. And you expressed the longing for a child…"Rick explained, but he could not continue. Sonia understood and covered his mouth with hers. She was overcome, consumed. When she came up for air she could only muster "I waited too long and can no longer bear a child. I had given up on that dream, but now…I have a daughter!!! Oh Ti Amo!!" She was laughing and crying at the same time.

It was several minutes before she regained her composure. Once she settled, she explored the master suite. She was stunned once again…there was a huge 4 poster bed, breathtaking windows and large glass doors. The bath was equally grand with a large garden tub and an equally large 4 head steam shower. She flopped on the bed to take it all in, but then she saw the pool. Outside the open doors children were playing in the yard. He snuggled beside her and pointed, saying "The girl with the dark curls in the purple dress is Gina." She locked eyes with him, so many questions sprang to mind "Can I? Does she know? What do I say?" she said, all at once.

He calmed her, " Say 'Ciao, sono Sonia, la tua nuova Madre, andiamo a vedere la tua camera da letto.' Hi, I am Sonia, your new mother, come see your bedroom. She knows of us and was given an idea that this day might come. The ladies considered this when we decided the wedding was happening. She was actually the flower girl in our wedding. I know it was a blur, but you will see, she is in all of the major pictures. Come on." As he guided her to her feet, she slapped him and kissed him, "You jerk! You know so much! Things I don't even admit to myself, you know them and just do them. Where did you come from? I never knew men like you were a real thing.Thank you my love! Let's go and see our daughter!"

As he walked slowly, she called out to Gina, the little lady waved and ran to them. Sonia dropped to her knees, as Gina approached, she wrapped her in a hug and kissed her cheek. After the embrace Gina complimented the home and yard, Sonia looked into her eyes forgetting what she was told to say. "Mia Figlia" blurted from her lips. Gina's lip quivered, managing only to say "Oh Madre!" and she clung to Sonia like a spider monkey. Sonia stood taking her by the hand and walked her into the house. As they entered, she was oblivious to items from the villa being carried in and set up for her. Furniture was being placed thoughtfully in the rooms and the ladies had begun cooking, She had tunnel vision, and all she saw was that this little girl and her small trusting hand in hers. She could not wait to bring her into the perfect room, made just for her.

They bonded instantly, they talked and played with dolls for the next several hours. When they finally emerged, a lunch was laid out on the dining table. The men had finished all of the moving and were enjoying paninis with wine, olives and dates out by the pool. The women were gathering around the table cackling like happy hens. All at once they spoke to Sonia and Gina, giving advice and compliments competing to be heard. Rosa slammed a hand on the table demanding "Ladies, please!" she proclaimed, then she formally welcomed Sonia as her new niece and daughter!

They all sat as one, little daughters with their mothers or older sisters. Gina sat happily with Sonia. Each woman helped her daughter with the meal, the team work was something only in stories for Sonia. The feelings filled her with excitement and a bit of stress! She had so much to learn... she thought "What happens if I fail? I have a child to care for and raise..." As if Rosa could read her mind, she said "Child, we are here to help you, teach you and make you a real Cicce woman," with a big hug.

Everyone finished lunch and began the clean up, at the same time Rosa took charge of prepartions for dinner. The men began work to restore the bocci court so they could play. They drank wine and smoked cigars.

Rosa ran the kitchen like a general as Vito directed the men. Some of the women tended to the needs of the men, others wrapped up lunch. The rest started to work at the dinner preparaations. The girls were separated by age, the young ones at the side of their mothers, the older ones given tasks within their ability. One 5 year old was even making bread! The oldest girls watched the infants and toddlers, what an organized group and all were so content with their position within the team.

The men and boys were no different, Vito ran the show with Rick and Carmine at his side. Rick was conducting the clean-up while Carmine inspected and prepped the game materials. The boys were assigned similarly except for the smallest ones, they were with the older girls. Before they knew it the three courts were clean, raked and set up. Vito had worked to organize the matches and sort out who was going to make it to the final brackets. It was set like a major sporting match. The men joked and "grab assed" like big kids.

As the matches started the ladies had most things in motion for dinner. The girls were given tasks to watch over sauces and everything was simmering for the main meal. The ladies and small children cheered for the men as they played. This was tradition for decades and now Sonia was part of it. Rick ran back and forth to kiss and support Sonia. The day rolled with such ease and joy, as the players were eliminated they began setting tables outside that resembled a huge banquet facility. The men paired off with their ladies as all but the final competitors began dinner presentation, olives, cheese, crostini, thinly sliced cold meats and so many different pickled vegetables. Such abundance! How will they have room for dinner?

Everyone relaxed again as they began to nibble and sip wine. Nobody was gorging and everyone was sober. Sonia felt as if she was living an *actual* Fairy Tale. She had never been so relaxed. Even the loud banter didn't phase her; it wasn't fighting, it was simply how they communicated. The Bocci tournament wrapped up with one of the teen boys against an elder uncle. It was close, but 'Crazy Uncle Charlie' was the victor! Laughter, cheers and joking ensued from all directions. They then moved to the tables as the wine flowed and salads were served.

The dinner went like everything else had, so relaxed that Sonia had forgotten this was her house warming. The meals, the family, the fun of all of it, and now her own husband and daughter. As the cleanup finished and everyone had left, the reality was a bright light. She had never gotten a little girl ready for bed, never mind seeing her eyes shine with new love. As she tucked Gina in, those little arms were *so* tight around her neck.

They exchanged gentle kisses goodnight. She walked out and shone from within.

Seeing her so content in their new home and family showed Rick how *right* it all was.

Rick went to shower, Sonia followed him in with a warm kiss, cooing

"Hold me, just love me!" They gently soaped and caressed each other under the steaming water like it was washing away the scars of their pasts. They had never had another like this, the bliss building was truly theirs to enjoy throughout their lives. They dried and went to bed as true husband and wife, the pleasure of just being one felt so extraordinary.

CHAPTER 9

Morning started brand new for Sonia, she was greeted with "Mattina Mamma!", a hug and kiss from sweet little Gina. The shift from the morning passion that had been spoiling her was exciting in a different way. The two ladies bounced to the kitchen as Rick was dressing for morning meetings. Gina went directly to peel oranges as Sonia collected bread, eggs, cheese and Capicola. As the pot whistled Sonia prepared Rick's tea while little Gina poured juice, what a little helper she was! Sonia just *had* to bend and kiss her, "Oh Ti Amo!!" Without a word Gina wrapped her little arms around her and held her. Quietly, she whimpered, "Mia madre."

Rick walked in, without interrupting the embrace, rather, he joined, "Mia Familia!!! Oh, um and I am pretty sure breakfast is ready." He said. The moment broke and the girls went back into action, Gina ushered Rick to the table where his tea, juice and fruit were waiting. As Sonia brought his favorite egg delight he scooped up Gina to place her on his knee, she smiled widely as he fed her a piece of orange. It was one bite for her and one for him, when Sonia brought hers over Gina traded to share hers with him too. "What a natural father he is" she thought, never was this conceived in her imagination. A chirp of that damned phone broke the mood, he finished quickly, kissed the girls and he was off.

Sonia and Gina sat like old friends as they finished eating and worked together to pick up before it was time for them to get cleaned up and dressed. They worked so smoothly together without any direction, "What a little 'grown up'", Sonia admired lovingly. As they finished she took Gina by the hand to the bathroom, they brushed their teeth, washed their faces and brushed their hair. Sonia put her hair up in a ponytail, as Gina watched. Then she scooped her up to set her on the counter managing her curly locks into the same look. Gina looked in the mirror, "Oh mi piace! Grazie."

Off to Gina's closet, Sonia found a perfect little country dress that resembled one of hers. She carried it to her room with Gina in tow, as Sonia removed her dress to demonstrate, Gina began donning her dress. The two matched so well, "Andare, della citta?" Sonia asked, nodding happily, Gina ran for her shoes. As Sonia slipped on her traditional black flats she ran back in with her little handbag. "Ok, andiamo!", and out they went to the new little Fiat that Rick had delivered for her a few days earlier.

With Gina in the back seat they were off, zipping along the country roads without a care as Gina sang a sweet tune. As they came into town everyone waved. Parking, she noticed a man she recognized as security who opened her door while another opened Gina's. The girls were escorted to the market and melted into the bustling community. "Mattina Madonna Cicce " was the new greeting every turn, what an honored title. All of the clerks and owners knew what she liked and might be interested in trying. The dress shop was no exception, as they walked in there were three of the nicest matching outfits for her and Gina. Gina ran in and out of the dressing room faster than Sonia could keep up with her, dancing in the mirror as Sonia would come out each time. Four skirts, four tops, and four dresses later… mission accomplished!

Sonia offered Gina to select dinner options, what a surprise the little master had in mind. She went directly to the fish man, filling her basket with mussels, a tray of calamari, and a large whole fish, "Branzini!" she exclaimed. Sonia was somewhat concerned inside, but she went along with her plans. As they drove home Gina rambled about her new clothes, the people, snacks and dinner.

When they got home, Gina ran from the car to the kitchen with her arms full of food. Sonia collected the other items and made her way into the house. She could hear Gina singing to the radio she had turned on and the sound of water running. What a sight, Gina was standing on a chair rinsing the fish to prepare for dinner. Sonia let her work as she watched, while caring for the other items. The 'piccolo pro' did the vegetables next as the time ticked slowly, soon it was 17:00 and Sonia knew she had to get things going.

Sonia stepped in to start on the garlic and white wine for the mussels, the water for the pasta and the oil for the fish. Sonia breaded the calamari under Gina's direction while the Branzini was soaking in the salt. In went the calamari, muscles and pasta. The scents filled the house like the spring air coming through the breeze. The sounds, smells, sensation, views, and *him* walking through the door with flowers in his hand and kisses on his lips filled her heart.

A kiss on Gina's forehead and one on Sonia's warm mouth sealed the welcome, "I am going to get out of this suit, you two are incredible!" he said. As he returned the calamari, olives and hard cheese were set on the table with a glass of wine. The pasta and mussels were just finishing as the fish went in, this would have been one of the best meals in any restaurant for Sonia, but this was a Monday dinner at home!!

In minutes they were all at the table, somehow Gina found her way to Rick's knee again. "Oh Poppa, this is so nice, I love that you love me," she cooed. He couldn't resist a warm hug as he fed her a mussel and bite of pasta. "She could melt an iceberg' he thought. He had lived a hard defined life up to this point, but *she* zipped straight to his heart. As Gina rambled about their outfits and the day spent aas mother and daughter, Sonia swelled with wonderment of her new family joy. She moved a little closer so the three were almost one, working their way through dinner with fun banter and so much happiness. As they finished dinner the girls each kissed one of his cheeks and cleared the table, as Sonia prepared a cappuccino Gina scraped plates.

Sonia arranged the chairs all three together and cut just one piece of olive oil cake, with three spoons. She added a large scoop of marscapone and they were just about ready. A glass of cold milk for Gina, Rick and Sonia shared the coffee, but they all shared the cake as one. Who knew dolce could be so much fun? There promised to be years of this ahead of them.

After hours of reading together and taless of everyone's day it was time for the ladies to get a bath. Rick could hear them giggle and splash, wishing this would never end and knowing he had one last trip to Rome to finish his career. Sonia had to know of the trip, but the details had to be top secret. He was going to tell her of a meeting in Rome tomorrow and that he should be back in 48 hours. The Rome cell had to be smashed for any hope of safety for the next few years. His teams was in place, the target and hit times were confirmed. He was to fly in tomorrow morning at 09:00 for a Vatican meeting at 10:30, Intel said the ambush would be just before the gates. The Swiss guard was ready and would have the gates secured so they can create a hammer and anvil effect. If they can't capture them they all must die horribly in public!

Suddenly the girls bounced from the bathroom smelling of shampoo and lotion. "Buona Notte Poppa!" she cried, giving a big hug and off she ran, to bed. As they left, he decided on a quick shower and glass of bourbon to "get his head right". As he exited the shower and dried, Sonia entered offering his drink. He hung the towel and took the drink as she began kissing down his chest and belly. As her knees hit the floor his cock was bouncing at her lips, she slowly stared into his eyes and her mouth went to work. So deliberate and intense as his eyes rolled, nearly shaking. She leaned back, "Come to bed and love me" she said as she dropped her robe.

She scooted to the bed and crawled teasingly, shaking that incredible tush, "Cum and get it!" He approached with her backing to him, the heat of her was swollen, red and drenched. As he touched her, she shuddered, when his cock parted her lips she gasped, pushing back to take more. Every dripping stroke made her gasp and buck until her first rupture. Falling to her belly he flipped her to her back. With those fabulous legs falling open, again she accepted every inch deep and full. In short order her legs clamped like a vice as she soaked them both. In a relentless pace he delivered the passion she craved until they both found their euphoria. Collapsing together, he crawled into the bed as she remained latched on to him, without separating they drifted into slumber.

As morning approached his internal clock went off at 04:00, sneaking out of bed he prepared for the day quiet as a mouse. As he armed up, he knew how serious the success of this mission was. He left without alerting her. He wrote a quick note refusing to admit that it may be his last. He had let it known to her that he is the assassin of the communists. He left it on the pillow and kissed her softly. As he crept down the hall a soft voice called "Poppa," he entered in the soft moon light. "Oh mia figlia, Te Amo! I have to work for the next three days, but I **will** be coming home, I promise!"

"Oh poppa, no morte! Prego! Ti Amo!" she cried. He squeezed her tightly, whispering "I promise!" She kissed his cheek and she matched his squeeze, "Oh poppa, kill them all!" It was like she had a window into his mind. He had given no clues, but she *knew*, did she have *the vision*? It was a "thing" in the Italians, regardless, he was intent on proving any thought of his death wrong! Rick broke the embrace with a kiss to her forehead, and tucked her back in.

As he sped to the plane it was time to clear his head, he couldn't miss a thing today. As he pulled up two of his team greeted him, "Hey brother, one last win!" Joey boasted. With a hand shake and chest bump they boarded. As they sat, the maps came out and the review began. Step by step they reviewed, from when they hit the ground to every turn along the route. Rick was in charge. He said "Remember we have a 'rat in the wood pile'. Remember who knows these plans. Remember who gets out without a scratch and who dies in the first contact!"

"I have the list, there are only 8 of us: me, Joey, Maria, Tommy, Carl, Jonny, Laura, and you! If there is a rat, we will know! I trust all of us." Joey was confident but he also knew that in order for the mission to work, the rat *had* to be taken care of! Final checks as those on the ground reported in. They were landing in 10. The all did a final weapons check. It was on!

The tires skipped the tarmac and it was time. Pulling into the hanger there were three different cars waiting for them. As they went down the stairs a strange face met them. Rick eyed her as she issued keys, then he got *that* look. He was given a red Corvette, Joey a Fiat, and Tommy an Audi. Without hesitation, Rick ordered "Lock her up! We need three new cars!" They all got into the Fiat, and sped off to a rental place.

Obtaining three "Plain Jane" cars they were off in three different routes. Within minutes each had a tail, as they approached known link ups at intersections, Maria was the only member unaccounted for. Closing on the Vatican his heart raced, a single transmission, "Get ready!" As he rounded the second to last turn a car darted across to block him!

Foot to the floor he smashed the driver's door watching his head explode on the "B- pillar", he had obviously stabbed the airbag to prevent activation. Gun fire erupted, from cars and ground locations, Rick's windows were already down to limit the glass frag. Shooting the first two he could ID he spun to go on the assault, one shooter began to run on the sidewalk. No second thought, car versus gun, car always wins! His instinct proved correct, run him down. And run him down he did!

Cars spun, shots from every direction, the counter sniper team crushed it in seconds. As the shots began to quiet Rick began to gasp and feel weak, he said out loud "Ahh shit! No time to die!" Pulling to the gate he fell from the car, the Pontifical Swiss Guard sprang to his side. The last thing he felt was the sign of the cross on his forehead as a young man began to pray. Time passed with no understanding, visions of Sonia, Gina, his mother and father, some evil creatures and bright light.

From a distance there was a voice yelling "Breathe you sum-na bitch! You are not dying today!" Rick's eyes fluttered under the bright lights and noises, he muttered "What the Fuck?" as his eyes rolled back in his head. Darkness, silence, then a harsh slap to his face brought him back "Hey-Hey! Stay with us! I hear you have ladies waiting for you. No little bullet can kill you, who is your wife, Sonia or Gina?" the doctor barked. "How do you know this??" Rick shouted as he grabbed the doctor's hand. "Are YOU the rat?!" He asked squeezing the man's wrist as if to crush it.

"Don Cicce! You have been calling out to them! I want to call them!" the kind doctor pleaded as prayers filled the background. Rick released his grip on the man, "NO! Never! They must not know anything until this is over!" he commanded. He saw many blurry figures but then a familiar young priest came into focus, he spoke with authority "Don Cicce, you are in the Vatican Hospital. The power of God surrounds you with His greatness! Now sleep and heal."

With that Rick allowed himself to sleep, such dreams filled his mind. The occasional opening of his eyes reminded him of those praying and working for the Lord's Blessing to BE. What felt like hours was actually days... "Good morning, what time is it?" his voice startled those in the room. "It's Thursday, and we love you!" two excited and relieved but still soft voices responded. "You are such a bad man, this is how you bring us to the Vatican?" Sonia teased as she rubbed his head. "Oh poppa, come home," Gina's soft voice pleaded.

"My loves, you shouldn't be here, it isn't safe. Who told you?" he whispered. "We saw it on the news, Gina told me you may die after you left. When we saw the story she *knew* it was you. We went to Vito and Father Luca, they got us here in secret. We are staying here, with you! It was reported that everyone is dead. But Joey said they have Maria, and she is talking!" Sonia reassured him.

Moments later Ambassador Sabastino entered the room, "May I? It is an honor to be here. The heroism of you and your team are the things of legend. I am here to inform you that you are now retired with full pay. Italia and the world are in your debt."

"Thank you sir, this is the end, NOW it is time for family!" Rick reinforced. An unimposing man entered the room, "WELL NOW! I guess I can still be called a doctor, the lord did great work." As Rick struggled with the right response the man chuckled, "Call me Father Marc, I was a doctor before dedicating my life to God. When I was told what was going to happen and the security required I went to work turning this area into a small hospital. Thank the Lord for a great medical community who helped with no questions asked."

"I need to go home, how long am I stuck here?" Rick inquired. "Well, a sucking chest wound, collapsed lung, several additional gunshots and you just want to get up and go home...I should have expected nothing less! If everything stays good, your family has a helicopter to pick you up tomorrow with medical staff on board and staff to be at your side," Father Marc replied.

"Then home tomorrow it shall be! Thank you Father and everyone who made this possible. Pray with me? "Our father..." Rick began, and everyone joined without a second thought. They all stayed together through the night, the Swiss Guard set up cots for the ladies and stood watch fit for a king. The next morning came with the best of love. Time to go home!

CHAPTER 10

The bird arrived and they flew them directly to Messina, where the Family
Security Team was waiting. They loaded Rick into the most unassuming
ambulance ever, with a very plain escort team. His ladies rode with him,
gabbing the entire way, nothing but happiness filled the ride. And soon,
home they were, the house was surrounded with the best Private Army
in the world. Coming inside Rosa was waiting with every aspect covered,
Rick wanted to walk but Oh NO!" the doctor refused. So wheeled in he
was, directly to their room where he climbed into bed with Sonia and
Gina on either side.

Rosa followed with some light snacks and drinks, "This is what family
is about!" he thought. As they snacked and snuggled, the fruits of their
labor were clearly displayed. "You ladies have made my life more than I
ever could have expected. We shall build on today for years of tomorrows!"
was the best way he could put it. In a short time the two women in his
life were sound asleep beside him, feeling safe and secure. He savored the
moment then suddenly realized that he had no phone or emails to manage.
He realized Family Business must stay below the radar, they must maintain
the safety they enjoyed today every day.

Plans began to run through his head, a major meeting of the key Families is still on in just two weeks. He thought, "The loss of unity can never happen, we MUST remain united. In a world where division is pulling to take from those who have worked for it in ways like never before. The main focus must be to 'keep everyone pulling the wagon and not let them into the wagon.' This is the simplest concept of leadership, everyone working for the common goal and never being carried by the others."

Rick knew that his family was the best example of this success, no one should ever come between that. Italian society was one of the first to realize the spiral, noticing the dwindling population and their youth departing the country for a lazier way of life. They saw it was easier to take and not contribute. Easier has consequences. This will never be allowes to happen in his family and he must stay dedicated in order stop it in his world. Those surrounding him only reinforced this dedication. Closing his eyes at last, he could relax in the love of his ladies, drifting off himself as their warmth surrounded him.

As dinner time neared Gina woke, as she moved about Sonia woke too. The duo quietly snuck to the kitchen to start dinner, Sonia selected a simple favorite of Rick's, pasta with garlic and olive oil. So basic, just like his outlook, Gina requested some bread, sliced sopressata and sharp cheese, "My dear, Poppa would love that too, can you take care of that?" Nothing had to be said, she just grabbed a chair, the items from the fridge, and a sharp knife. Yes only in the old country can such a little girl be trusted to do such, in a moment she had everything cut and arranged on a plate.

As Sonia drained the pasta the unmistakable sound of a cane thumped into the cucina, "Ciao mia belles!" Sonia helped him sit and poured some chilled 'acqua frizzante' with a kiss. Gina hurried over with the meat, cheese, and olives which she delivered with a hug. He thought, "This is the life! Preservation of this simplicity is a huge task but worthy of my every effort."

As they sat closely, enjoying the simple dinner Sonia was reminded of a similar experience as a small girl. She remembered the sparkle in her mother's eyes as they would gather at the table. Family dinner, how had she lost sight of the importance of such things? She hadn't understood that there had been a void in her life, a need. Nothing in her hugely successful life had ever fulfilled her. It all made sense now. She had lost sight of this basic need as a foundation within our society. This spoke volumes about how the change to our core values had started! Now, she understood, doing her part at home and in her community was her true mission, now and forever.

Focused unity grew from that point, over the next several months they worked as a well oiled machine. It was so easy, and with Rick's steady recovery nothing was a chore. Gina grew with them too, the large family gatherings were a constant and had positive impact. The family led the community by example. Gina was starting school in the fall, they were known as such a great asset to the community, and the small school welcomed Sonia as volunteer. Her efforts helped to prepare Gina too, giving her time to meet the teachers and other children. Sonia intended to continue volunteering and shaping the next generations.

This was the plan for long term success, so simple but complex and beneficial for all. Rick had become heavily involved with the local and state policia, supporting them with training at the highest levels. Their combined efforts created a bridge that The Family had never known. They were fully accepted as legitimate by law enforcement for the first time in over a century. Select world wide efforts continued based on what Rick and Sonia had started. Everything locally was driven with renewed efforts of continuity.

Then an unexpected guest arrived, Cousin Gaetano knocked at the door. Gaetano is a prison warden at the largest facility in Sicily and had his ear to everything that happened in the underworld. They had not seen each other since they were boys, but both had a great respect for the journey of their careers. This visit was of great importance, Gaetano spoke solemnly "My cousin, you have made great enemies in your life, this message had to be delivered in person. The communists and Calabrese have joined to kill you once and for all. Your work uniting the families here and in the South have impacted the businesses of the Calabrese, and your work with the police has them enraged. Even the Vatican walls have eyes and ears, the gunfight at the gate is what legends are made of. They are planning a full assault on you and our family to send a message in both directions. I have a plan but I need your help."

"My cousin, your loyalty is what legends are made of, we will win this too. Are you safe in your position? Are you keeping the Calabrese unrestricted in the facility? I will fortify everything here and in the community as a whole," Rick reassured. "I live in the facility with my family now, my staff is trustworthy. We are being smart about keeping the Calabrese unrestricted so they will keep talking, this will all change once the necessary actions are in motion. The family must not 'tip our hats' to what we know to be slick about what you do here. You have many communists in the area, some even working for you. Here is a list of those we have identified. I also have Agents in the best units of the Federal Police working around the country. I have a plan that will require the best coordination. You are the guy to lead it!" Gaetano explained.

Sonia had slipped away when she heard the first mention of communists, but she stayed close enough to hear the conversation. Gina was occupied playing. Rick anticipated this and moved the conversation to the garage. He asked "What is our timeline?" Gaetano responded, "Three to five days, not much but enough. We have the right guys, resources and equipment. This is the only place where we can be seen together, this burner phone is clean and has all of the key contacts already loaded. I have the Federal and Corrections teams ready to go at a moment's notice. When the first assault starts here those teams will hit their leadership, we already have the Intel and warrants. We are not in this for prisoners and that is where you come in! As they present, take them out, use those sniper teams and assault teams you have been training. But you can't use any of your old teams, they have too many rats. Word is that your buddy Joey is no buddy, in fact he is on his way to see you. Joey is the bait to draw you out, where the meet will be is the start of the war. When you hear from him you know what to do, just let me know the date and time. I know you will handle everything here, when the meeting time marks we will have our coordinated raids. We are keeping eyes on every single member of their leadership, the communist coordination including Joey gives us International Charges!"

Rick understood, saying "I knew this day would come, the teams on the police and family side all have their assignments and equipment. I will get warning orders to each leader only to prevent any OpSec leaks, these are the best guys I have known since the Army days. Joey was once one of the best, I have have had my suspicions though.

What a shame, I know you haven't been down this heavy road but you are a great man! Good luck my cousin, we need to stay much closer after all of this is over. Our futures are bright."

As Gae walked to the car Rick recognized the Security Team set out over hundreds of meters. As the car drove away Rick went to the secret safe behind the toolboxes, he began checking weapons, collecting equipment and planning what to say to his girls. He strapped on his favorite 320 and 365, they had never failed him and had several wins. He stopped to gaze on Sonia's .38, he had never wanted her to need it again, but it was necessary. She would need some extra training. Once in the house he laid everything out and set up his computer, the cryptic message was drafted…Now, send! "Here we go!" that same old voice blurted out. Sonia entered the kitchen with Gina at her side, understanding, Sonia began to cry. Crying had left her persona since she was a girl, "Awe, shit!" she sobbed. Gina stood amazingly calm and strong, "Mamma, Poppa has this one under control. I know this, he will win again, I promise."

"How? What? Gina?" Sonia was so confused by the calm of the child. "My dear, she has the sight. Not that I am going to get over confident, but she knew I was going to die on that last one. She told me and it gave me the strength to win. I will never check up but we must have faith. I am going to give you my best, forever; but today we must train for tomorrow!" With that he began reviewing how to stand, manipulate the pistol, grip, sight alignment, trigger control, click, click, and repeat. And repeat they did until she was rock steady, loading and unloading the dummy rounds like a pro with those old school speed loaders.

"Hone,…. I hate this but I love that you are here for us this way. The danger I was always warned of is real and was kept from me by courageous people like you. Never stop loving us!" Sonia pleaded. A big hug and kiss said it all, Rick responded, "Now let's get you loaded up, Sabby and Carla are coming to visit. Yes I know they work for me, but they are your team now until this is over."

Things moved at light speed, messages, Sabby and Carla, guns, radios, police of all types like Sonia had never seen. Gina remained calm, playing with Carla and her daughter Sissy. Normal and insane all at once, Sonia had never seen anything like this. She kept the coffee, snacks and everything else coming as needed.

A couple of days into it the expected call came from Joey. He acted like the great old friend that had been trusted on so many successful missions. They had never failed until the last one. Joey was the only one in the fight who emerged without a scratch, but today he had urgent info that had to be passed in person! The message gave a coordinate and a time for 21:00 tonight, it was on!

Pulling it up, there was a small church right in the center of town. Rick always loved churches as link ups, so many ways in and out to stay fluid. It was the church where they were married. Father Luca couldn't be part of this. Or was he? Many in the church had become socialist minded in recent years and he could communicate without suspicions.

Messages went out to everyone, especially Gae. Father Gino had retired but had the trust of the family since Rick was a boy, turning to Sabby he said, "Get someone on Father Gino ASAP, I must talk to him!" Guns had always been left out of the church, sadly, this was all about to change. There was a young man who had been an associate for years who resembled Father Luca and could pass for him at a distance. A message went out, "Get Leo, lock down Father Luca quietly and get Leo in his place now, dress Assunta as a nun and get her in there too!"

Thirty minutes later, "Father Leo" and "Sister Assunta" were in place; the "altar boys" were in the confessionals, the chior loft, and sanctuary. The perimeter teams for all of the houses reported in, the police leadership was ready for the church as they watched for Joey, unusual movements, and any strangers coming in.

20:30 came, time to "saddle up and get it on!" Rick kissed the girls and off he went, the lights dimmed as she watched. His phone and radios chirped constantly, his guys gave the signal of 2 flashes of red light as he proceeded. As he closed on the church he passed three occupied parked cars, no flashes. The police descended, the first two cars were nothing, the third erupted in gunfire.

It had begun, another car flashed the headlights 5 times, the old team signal. It was Joey! Rick drove past, into the rear of the secured church bolting into the rear door. Taking up a position at the altar, he waited. The doors cracked as Joey entered, "I am alone! No guns! I am not responsible for those guys in the car. We all are compromised, I need your help!" Joey slowly came into the light, hands outstretched. As the door latched, the gunfire right outside, Joey hit the floor of the aisle.

"Crawl up here!" Rick called. Joey did as told as the stone church shielded them from the bouncing shots. Leo search and cuffed him. Joey complied without issue, "We need to get out of here!" Seconds later the clear signal came from the perimeter team, a message came that Luca gave up the goods, Joey was dirty and needed to get into the chair.

Leo and Assunta threw Joey in the truck, they all mounted up and went to the "Fish House". There was so much history there, the most secure location for meetings, questioning and fitting heavy shoes for eternal swims. As they pulled up the door opened, they all drove straight in. The perimeter team was bolstered, expecting a tracker on Joey and they were right. As the doors began to close they came from everywhere trying to get in. Over the years the place had been armored and the doors powered, for fun as the last guy tried they let him live so the doors would crush him slowly (turns out he was a Deacon in the church for Luca).

The external team worked exceptionally with support from guys inside moving to roof positions. With the sound of claymores, 240's and 249's humming Rick was calm, that was the music of victory. They "drug" Joey by his feet to a large oak chair in the middle of the room, strapping him in. All the while Joey had been silent, eyes closed, he quietly said, "I knew it would come to this, I had to do it, I was ordered."

"By who big mouth? Either they will kill you fast or I kill you slow. If you satisfy me I may let you live! Take off his shoes!" Rick barked. His shoes were yanked off, and tourniquets placed on each extremity. Rick checked a strange looking shotgun, a large fish hung next to him, he turned and shot it. Joey's imagination ran wild, "I have seen you kill but not like this, all the good times, the fights we won! DC! DC sent the orders for the SA trip, the Vatican and this one. Really!" Rick took a large piece of tire tread, placed it over Joey's right foot and put the muzzle to it. "OK! Ok, not everything came from DC but it was cleared with DC, trust me!" Blam!!! The blast shattered his foot, "*That* will never work again!" Rick stated, viewing the crushed appendage.

"I was under cover with them, it had to look right but we always knew you had everything covered," Joey grunted. "Names!" Rick commanded, setting the tire on the other foot, "5, 4, 3, 2," Blam!! Joey howled in pain as the other foot was shattered. "My family you Fuck!" Rick was interrupted by messages. "I see, get all of the bodies, the Federal Police will want them. Yes, Gaetano has them all locked down and is going to the question there too, the Calabrese should be running like rats. The Vatican? Really? the

Swiss Guard has the Pope and the Congress of Cardinals has spoken to return to follow the bible?! Hell yes!" He returned his focus to Joey. "Want to live? Start talking! Knees are next!"

"It was Astin! Gen. Astin, he is the director of all of this, I have recordings, written orders! I saved. I can get prosthetic feet, please don't take my knees." Joey sobbed. Rick took a pistol from a table, checked it and put it to Joey's forehead. "You and those turds don't deserve to live!" Rick cocked the hammer and angled it up slightly as he dropped the hammer. Pow, the blank went off burning a streak down his scalp and lighting some hair on fire. With a giggle Rick threw a bucket of water to put out the fire.

Pleased, Rick said, "Bandage him up, the Feds are coming!

CHAPTER 11

They collected Father Luca and Joey, returning them to the steps of the church, where they left them handcuffed, shackled, gagged and blind folded. They used Sodium Pen on them to put them in a stuporous and honest state. The Fish House and the church were sanitized, but the police weren't even interested. When they arrived they simply threw them in a van, asked if we had any casualties and left. The scene at the Fish house and family homes was similar, the bodies were collected and no casualties were reported.

A simple message from Gaetano said, "With the understanding of treason charges everyone in custody talked. The Calabrese raids were huge, watch the news!" By that afternoon reports of raids in Austria, Switzerland, Hungary, Poland, the Czech Republic and Greece were significant. Several incidents resulted in gun battles with the suspects, however Germany, France, Britain, and the US took no action. This made it very clear the validity of Joey's admissions, especially when the Pope suddenly retired and returned to South America.

The Cardinals took swift action to re-establish the foundation of the church in the mandates of the bible. Father Gino and several other retired priests returned to the church as quality leaders again, who were supported by the Vatican. The church openly identified enemies of the 'Western Values' to root them out.

Community leaders came forth as well, no known Socialist with Communist ideals was able to hide now. The country was coming back together, the families wasted no time supporting the new stability. Uncle Vito was asked to take over as the mayor, which he accepted happily. Rick was offered a position within the Carbonari, which he declined, opting to remain as a consultant.

As the family business stepped back out of the public eye, Rick and Sonia could resume their lives, enjoy their status, and raise their daughter. That night they all went home to Rosa's, the feast put out in the courtyard rivaled that of a Roman Emperor. Every sort of food and drink overflowed, the children played with great happiness while the warriors of the night before nursed their wounds. Rick was so proud of the effort made by his team members, throughout wars with the Army and his later years in the Agency he had never had such a flawless group.

Recognizing this he stood and raised a glass, "I have been blessed with so much in my life, today I have the grace of God surrounding me in the presence of St. Michael's best. SALUTE!" The glasses waved and the cheers burst. As the celebratory dinner wrapped up the events and lack of sleep kicked in, turning to his ladies "Andiamo mi amore, la casa. Buono Sera mia FAMILIA!"

With that the girls ran to the car, ready to leave by the time Rick was in the car. Arriving home, the girls knew to wait until Sabby and Carla greeted them. Sonia and Gina presented them with food and drink from the party, they thanked them and they all went to the kitchen.

Rick gave them each an envelope before retiring for a shower, Sonia brought him a glass of bourbon and turned down the bed. Sonia was waiting, as he got in bed she kissed and caressed her man.

Getting comfortable she quickly put him to sleep, everyone was exhausted from the previous 36 hours. As morning came Rick woke at 04:30 to use the bathroom, returning to bed he found Sonia laying with her head off of the bed. As he approached she grabbed his hips pulling him to her, as the tip hit her lips she swirled it with her tongue before inhaling it. She accepted as much as physically possible with every stroke until it was a rock, when she was satisfied with what he had she spun on her back to accept him into her. Not a word was said, her body said everything as he filled her in the most satisfying way. Thrust after slow deep thrust she bubbled with pleasure, after a tremendous rupture she struggled to mumble "Oh my love!" Flipping her feet up she pulled him down to her waiting breasts, with a handful of his hair she steered him from one nipple to the other as their pace reached a fevered pitch. Together the became rigid the wave consumed them both.

Staying combined she pulled him into the bed where they fell back to sleep. The sun soon interrupted their slumber, the sound of little feet filled the house. Then came a soft knock, "Mamma, Poppa?" as the door cracked they waved her in. Gina and Sissy came in so carefully carrying trays with fruit, juice, toast and sliced meat. "Bene mattina" they said, as they set the trays down, a quick kiss and off they were to greet Sabby and Carla the same way. "This is real love isn't it?" Sonia asked. "Yes my dear, we have found it in every way!" Rick replied as fed her a grape.

This was only the beginning, day by day, kiss by kiss, every simple blessing shined in gold. Sonia had hit the lottery in a way she never expected, a man who truly loved her like no other, safety in a truly crazy world, an incredible child, everything she ever asked for. A life like no other. The time had come for Sonia to settle in and smell the roses. She was surrounded by so much. The world was genuinely at her doorstep!